# Claimed By Desire

# Claimed By Desire

KayAnna Kirby

Sovereign Press

First paperback edition 2011

ISBN: 978-0-983-41610-4

PRINTED IN THE UNITED STATES OF AMERICA

visit us at www.asovereignpress.com

*For Gregory,*
*My Knight in Shinning Armor*

# ACKNOWLEDGMENTS

There isn't enough room to thank all the friends and family who have helped me along the way, by listening, encouraging, and holding me to my deadlines.

Thank you Gregory for believing in me. I couldn't do it without you, you mean everything to me, plus you gave me the most awesomest (is that a word?) daughter on the planet.

A special thanks goes to Nadia for keeping me honest, encouraging me, and being such a great friend. Love you.

I am grateful to the bloggers and writers who share their time and effort in helping others (like me) find their voice, learn and grow. You are all invaluable.

# *ONE*

IF ALLISON DIDN'T FIND a bathroom within T minus two minutes, it would be a disaster. A life ending, never show her face in public ever again disaster. She pulled on the hem of her formal black dress and ran, walked, around the massive coliseum feverishly searching for the girls room, while balancing in her ill advised four inch heels. The marble floors were so shiny Allison realized, she could put her makeup on by it. Frantic and starting to lose patience as well as her inhibitions, she glanced at the ocean crashing on the deserted beach a few feet to her right. It was night time, practically pitch black outside. No one would see her if she went on the beach, would they? As if being pulled by a magnetic force, Allison migrated towards the open air columns that led to the white sand beaches of the Cayman Islands. Soon, this torture could be all over if only..

"Don't even think about it."

Allison gave her best friend Samantha a curt look and continued to drift towards the beach.

"Fine. Do what you want, but don't look to me for help when you stoop down and one of those tiny red crabs pinch you in your cooch--"

"Sam, shut up!" But it did the trick. The visual Sam gave her of a crab pinching her most sensitive area loosened the magnetism to the beach and Allison returned to the search for the little girls room at the coliseum; a massive and opulent structure designed for the get-togethers of the wealthiest people in the world.

"Yep, you'd never look at Joe's Crab Shack the same way again," said Samantha, shaking her head and knitting her eye brows at the same time. Allison looked over and realized she'd reached her breaking point. If she laughed like she wanted to, all the primping she'd done hours before would be for naught. So, she kicked off her silver and black Kenneth Cole shoes, grabbed them and ran along the marble floors barefoot until she finally found it.

Allison slipped her shoes back on and she could have sworn she heard the theme song from Rocky as she entered the ladies room. Safe. Samantha came in a few seconds later, fixing her lip gloss while she waited. Allison appeared with a relieved look on her face.

"That was quick," said Samantha. She didn't expect her friend to be finished so fast, with the way she was carrying on.

"All I had to do was pee." Allison washed her hands, patted down her hair as the humidity made hundreds of tiny strands dance around as if they were injected with electricity atop her head.

"Sam, I should have worn my hair up. This humidity is wreaking havoc on my hair," said Allison while walking out of the bathroom.

"Allison--"

"And why are these floors so slippery? You know I almost killed myself just now? What do they have, little oompa loompas spit shinning the floors every few hours? If I wasn't careful, I'd have slipped on the floor, my dress would have gone over my head and my jewels would be visible for all to see.--"

"Allison, calm down. Why do you always seem to over-react."

"It's a conspiracy. They're trying to ruin me."

Samantha laughed. "There's no you to ruin Kumquat. Before someone can ruin you, you have to have something to ruin."

"I have plenty... Kiwi-", but Allison had already lost. The game started around ten years ago when they became friends at RiverMont High School. Whenever either of them started behaving silly; either complaining a little too much, over-reacting, not reacting enough, or just being a total douche, the other one would call the other a Kumquat. No specific reason. The name sounded funny. Plus at fourteen, they could say Kumquat without getting in trouble and defend themselves by affirming that Kumquat was a fruit.

"Who are THEY? You know what, don't answer that. Allison! You have to calm down. Look at me." Samantha took Allison's arm and turned to face her. Although Sam was only five feet three inches tall, she held Allison's five foot eight frame at a standstill.

"No one is trying to ruin you. You look great, you are great at what you do, this will be a good night. You know what you're doing. You will go in to that ballroom, meet all sorts of important people, hob-nob with worldwide dignitaries, then go back to your hotel room, and get a good nights rest so you can hammer into these guys tomorrow. Nothing to it."

Samantha was usually the level headed half of the duo. Things didn't bother her as they bothered Allison, and she counted on her friend to ground her when her mind delved into airy nonsense. A couple passed by on the way to the reception and the look they gave the two girls, one tall and statuesque, one short and curvy looking lovingly into each others' eyes, made Allison and Samantha feel as if they each had two heads. Many people thought they were gay. Some who knew them and some who didn't. They didn't care, instead they proceeded to the party.

A warm summer breeze blew through the Colosseum type columns located all around them. The marble floors were polished to a high shine and light bounced off the torches lining the walls. The sound of crashing waves and the smell of the sea calmed Allison as she made her way to the annual, as she just found out, CEO's ball on the Grand Cayman Island in the capital, George Town.

Every year, the Titan's of businesses meet in the Cayman Islands, where their businesses are registered anyway, and party, or network as they like to call it. Lifestyles of the Rich and Famous had nothing on how these people lived.

"This is amazing Sam. I mean, who lives like this?" Allison, looked up and saw the biggest most opulent diamond filled chandelier she'd ever seen, or heard of.

"This place put someone back the annual GDP of Venezuela. Wow!"

"This *is* the Governor's palace, I guess they treat their leaders well in the Caymans. Although, I would think you should know what all of this cost and is worth, you are the one heading up the audit right?"

"Not on this place. My firm is doing a financial audit on Anderson properties only. I think the company is buying another development and they needed audited financial statements or something." Allison knew her friend and also knew she'd told Samantha this approximately eighteen times since she invited her to tag along for the trip. She never listened.

Allison went on, not because Samantha really cared about the particulars of her job, but because dealing with work calmed her, made her focus. Plus, Sam wouldn't remember anyway. She continued.

"Anderson Properties is buying one of the resorts on seven mile beach. Yours truly will audit their financials and make sure no one's overstating or understating their assets."

Samantha finished sending the text she was typing and put her phone in her tiny clutch bag.

"Mr. Osmund thought it was a good idea for me to come and meet some of the people I'm going to work with over the next week. He doesn't think I get out enough."

"Anderson properties? Who Bryson Anderson, Jr., the billionaire guy? Will he be here tonight?"

"Yeah that's him. I do not look forward to working with him. I hear, he's a real playboy. He spends money like water and feels like he's the King of the Universe."

"I'm waiting for the bad parts, I know it's there somewhere."

"Oh come on Sam, you're not serious. He's this, born with a silver spoon in his mouth, big baby. My boss told me specifically 'Whatever Mr. Anderson wants, Mr. Anderson gets."

"I still haven't heard anything I object to as yet."

"Alright. He's ruthless. When he's involved with a deal, you'd be lucky to leave with the shirt on your back."

"Alli, you're exaggerating--"

"I'm not. He swoops in and takes advantage of businesses on the brink of failure, buys them, fires everyone and starts over. " A triumphant look crossed Allison's face. Now her friend would understand.

"How about I pretend I'm you and sit in on, I mean with Bryson and do the audit. That way, you wouldn't have to deal with him.

"Yeah, and I'm a ripe Kumquat." They exploded in laughter.

They'd reached the ballroom. They could tell by the two fifteen foot lit torches on either side of a dark and heavy wooden door. Two men dressed in tuxedos blanketed the door. They showed their invitations to the men. Together the men unlatched a wooden latch, more fan fare than an actual lock, and ushered Allison and Samantha into a fairytale.

# *TWO*

THE CEILING OF THE ballroom was adorned with diamond chandeliers as far as the eyes could see. Between the chandeliers hung white see through drapes in a loop on the ceiling. All the elements in the ballroom came together to make it feel like the were no longer on earth, but a faraway, fantasy land.

Men were dressed in tuxedos and women were dressed in floor length ball gowns of every color imaginable. Reds, blues, and greens flowed around Allison as she stared at the scene in awe. An orchestra was playing classical music about three hundred or so feet directly in front of her, and a hardwood dance floor was erected directly in front of the orchestra where couples waltzed and swirled to the music.

A ten foot buffet table sat on the left wall of the ballroom, with shrimp, cheese, fruits, roast beef, lamb, and...

"Sam...Sam is that a pig with an apple in it's mouth?"

Samantha turned to look where Allison was pointing.

"Huh, what, where....Oh my, that IS a pig with an apple in it's mouth!"

"This is a little much," said Allison.

An usher dressed in a black tuxedo with a white bow tie and white gloves like the ones positioned outside the door bowed slightly to Sam.

"Madame, what party are you with, I can help you find your table."

"Oh, I'm just her friend along for the party, she's the registered guest," said Sam, pointing to Allison."

Allison turned to the maitre d', "I'm with Abbots, Glen and Notto, PC. "

"This way ladies," said the maitre d' as he ushered Allison and Sam to their table.

Allison and Samantha followed the maitre d' through the round tables in the ball room. Some people were drinking coffee, while others drank colorful alcoholic concoctions in martini glasses, wine glasses, and some cocktail glasses. Light feminine perfumes mingled with husky masculine scents as they made their way to their seats. Everyone was dressed in their Sunday best. Rich reds and gold saris' worn by the Indian heads of state, along with bold yellows and greens of the Nigerian royalty, mingled with Dior gowns and Armani suits.

Allison was overwhelmed with the amount of money in the room. She glanced down at her simple but elegant black strapless gown that she picked up on sale at Macy's and wondered if she looked as out of place as she felt. Could they tell her diamond earrings, necklace and bracelet, were bought as a set in the accessories department at Macy's' for twenty four ninety nine? It seemed like not even a pair of socks for these folks cost that little.

Too late to worry about that now. Allison pushed the thought from her mind, straightened her posture, held her chin up a little higher, and followed the maitre d'.

The AG&N table was filled, except for two seats spaced about three people apart.

"Oh shucks, we're not going to be able to sit together Sam. You're okay with that, right?"

"I'm a big girl, I'll be fine."

As Mr. Osmund saw Allison approach the table, he put his Jack Daniels and coke down, got up and strode over to her. At five foot six, two hundred and twenty pounds with an advanced case of male pattern baldness, Mr. Osmund looked like a penguin in his black tuxedo and white shirt, as he waddled his way over to meet Allison. A cute, squish-able penguin, but a penguin none the less. Allison had to bite her bottom lip to stop herself from snickering as she saw her boss approach.

"Allison, good of you to join us."

"I'm sorry Mr. Osmund. It won't happen again."

She gave him a sheepish grin that he didn't return. She heard him, like she'd heard him the last few weeks lecturing her about her less than stellar work habits.

"You're a great accountant Allison, but your tardiness and absence are unacceptable." If Mr. Osmund and her father weren't friends from college, she wondered if she would still have a job.

"Come, I want you to meet a few people." He hoped the opportunity to audit such a big and important client like Anderson Properties, to possibly further her career, and for once everything to go well, would give her the motivation she needed to recommit herself.

He introduced her to several potential clients, and observed how she dealt with them. She was smart, diligent, and didn't miss anything. That was one of the reasons she was valuable to the company. With his guidance, Allison had developed into a sharp CPA with a penchant for saving their clients money, streamlining their practices, and being a ruthless auditor. Until lately.

"Mr. Simmons, this is Allison Caine, our lead CPA on Anderson Properties."

"How do you do, Ms. Caine. It's a pleasure to meet you. I've heard much about you."

"I hope all good things. I wouldn't want to scare you away." Allison smiled as she shook Mr. Simmons hand and sat down at the seat with her name on the chair.

She's a live wire Mr. Osmund. This should be an interesting week." replied Mr. Simmons.

"Why is that?" asked Allison.

"Because I hear you will be working closely with Mr. Anderson, and he is, how do you say it... quite the character."

Trying to hide her annoyance at even the mention of Bryson's name, Allison nodded slightly and turned her attention to the striking woman to her right. That's how it went for the next forty five minutes. Small talk was exchanged with everyone around the table. Allison glanced over at Sam chatting with a woman in her late fifties. Catching small snippets of the conversation, Allison could have sworn she heard Sam discuss the merits of 1920s big band music versus todays popular music. Shaking her head, Allison excused herself and made her way to the buffet table.

How would Sam know about big band music. She was such a suck up.

Meat.

Allison wanted meat, and lots of it. The thought of it made her mouth water. Allison made her way through throngs of dignitaries and reached the buffet table and went to work.

*At least it's not carbs*, she thought.

Allison discreetly placed a respectable, at least to her, amount of sliced roast beef on her plate and proceeded to check out the lamb on the other side of the table. Not interested, she headed back to her table. Before she could get there, the back of a large tuxedo collided with her roast beef. Allison watched as her beloved protein somersaulted it's way to the marble floors. Slightly stunned that someone could be so clumsy and or careless she started to dread the walk back to the buffet table. Her feet were starting to swell in her four inch heels and she didn't know what to do.

Frustration bubbled in her veins. She didn't need this. All she wanted was her roast beef and come to think of it, a bed. Was that too much to ask?

"I'm sorry, I did not see you there. Don't worry about the mess, I'll have one of the matire d' take care of it," said *Mr. can't watch where he's going*.

With fire in her soul, Allison forced her eyes away from her beloved roast beef on the floor and searched for the deep husky voice of the culprit. If Allison wasn't so annoyed and frustrated, she might have found the voice sexy. Now, she was ready to kill.

For a second Allison considered her strong emotional response to the accident. After all, she wasn't a hot head. It was really no big deal. All she had to do was brush it off and either get more food, or move on. But a small beast stirred in Allison. She was hungry and wasn't going to take it anymore.

She stood straight up and stared at the man in front of her. She drew in a sharp breath and touched her hand to her mouth.

*OH MY GOD!*

Stunned into silence, Allison tilted her head up to meet the eyes of the six foot, three inch height of the man in front of her. His broad shoulders filled his tuxedo and took up her vision. All sound and movement disappeared around her. They became the only two people in the massive room.

His eyes glowed and his golden skin sparkled under the chandeliers. His masculine, strong face stared back at her in awe. He was gorgeous. Greek God gorgeous. As gorgeous as she remembered him. Commanding eyes, and strong features. His beautiful face placed on top of his big strong body sent familiar electricity racing down her spine. Thoughts of his hard, naked, body stretched out above her , as he traced his big rough hands down her body to rest on her nipples sent shivers through her body and liquid heat to her core. Just like that, she remembered being in his arms again, being claimed by him, body and soul. The force of the sensations made Allison's knees weak. When she felt herself wobble, she reached back to hold onto the chair behind her.

That momentary distraction snapped her out of her flashback. She shook her head slightly to clear any remaining thoughts that threatened to creep back into her consciousness, and armed herself with a steely exterior.

Allison grabbed his hand. A charge of electric heat stung her fingers and left butterflies making a home in her stomach. The erotic memories threatened to enter her consciousness once again. Shaking it off, she dragged him to a deserted corner of the ballroom while one of the maitre d' busied himself cleaning up the broken plate and roast beef. He followed with no resistance.

Reaching a distance far enough away to guard against eavesdroppers, Allison spun around with daggers in her eyes.

"What are you doing here? Is this some sort of sick joke?"

With a cool composure, betraying nothing, he bore into Allison with his eyes and a small smirk.

"I should ask you the same thing. Sorry for bumping into you back there, by the way."

She didn't want to be reminded about her hunger. Now, she couldn't decide what she was hungry for, food or something else.

"Look, I don't know what your problem is or why you're even here, but I am working. I really don't need someone I had---anyway, I don't need you here right now. What ever happened between us will have to be discussed at a later time. I mean, to ambush me at a working dinner is low, Buster." Anger flowed through her veins as thick and slow moving as mud.

But there was something else. Something she hoped did not show on her face and betray her.

Lust.

Her traitorous body wanted him to lift her up against the cold back wall, hike up her dress and fill her again and again, harder and harder, maybe even bite her nipples until she collapsed on him, sweating and spent from her peak.

"It's been a long time. Too long."

His eyes were distant for a moment. He was no longer there with her, but someplace else. His lips twitched slightly as he stared at Allison, and she wanted to reach up and capture them with her mouth. Allison stared as his tongue slowly swiped across his lips. He didn't seem like he realized what he was doing. She recalled him swiping his tongue along her soft lips, then enter her welcoming mouth. She was there for his taking.

"I've thought about you a lot." He moved closer. Allison could feel the heat coming off him. Almost as if he was surrounded by a force field, and with every step she was being drawn closer to him.

"The way you felt." He let out a breath bending to whisper in her ear. "Naked. Soft. Wet." He took another step forward. "I still remember your nipples getting hard in my mouth. I had to find out the easy way, you like to be bitten." He chuckled softly. He looked like he was having too much fun. Allison was frozen. He was strumming her libido with his words and he didn't seem like he was going to stop anytime soon. He advanced again.

"And you taste intoxicating. Your neck, nipples, and clit. Especially when you're cumming on my tongue." Allison couldn't believe he'd just said that. Her heart beat sped up, and her panties were getting wetter by the second. She was slammed by need so strong she started to swoon.

Allison instinctively backed up with every step he took toward her. Now she'd reached the wall and had no where to go but into his hard chest. She placed her palms behind her on the wall to steady herself and took a deep breath. Big mistake. A rush of cinnamon, spice, and cool summer breezes invaded her senses. She moaned by reflex. He smiled as if on cue. A wicked naughty smile. One that spoke of long sexy climactic nights.

Allison was lost in his golden eyes. He mesmerized her. Her temperature spiked. Her clothes felt binding, restrictive. She gained a moment of reprieve when her head brushed the wall behind her. The coldness cooled her down, slightly. When his hands moved to fix his pants, the heat started to rise again.

Their heartbeat and breath synchronized. He was so close, she smelled the peppermint candy he'd recently finished eating with a bite of whiskey behind it. The sweetness mixed with the alcohol was like an aphrodisiac to her. She couldn't get enough, but wouldn't let him know.

The air he breathed out caressed the outside of her dress, tickling her skin in all the right places, and her treasonous body responded with liquid fire and hardened nipples. She inhaled again, not sure if it was to help slow the pressure advancing between her legs, or to get more of that sweet, husky smell. Which ever it was, she parted her lips to say something, but nothing came out. She licked her lips to try again. His pants got tighter.

"That happened a long time ago. Long enough anyway."

He placed his right hand on the other side of her head.

"Maybe, what you need, is a reminder."

*What I need?* That snapped Allison out of the fast advancing seduction taking hold of her. She worked too hard to allow this man to tell her what she needed. She knows what she needs and that is not to make the same mistake she made almost two months ago, by bedding down with him again.

"Don't tell me what I need!" She placed both her hands on his hard chest and pushed. Nothing. She might as well have been pushing against an army tank.

"If I remember correctly, I can peg what you need pretty well--."

"Look, that was a mistake. Why don't you forget about it. Let's move on and please stop stalking me." Maybe he could, because she couldn't forget.

"I'm like an elephant, I don't forget anything. I'm like an elephant in another way, but I don't think you have forgotten that part."

*The arrogant bastard.*

"I've had enough. I'm leaving. You gave me enough of a parting gift that night."

Brushing past him, Allison ducked under his arms and walked back to her table.

Sam gave Allison a puzzled look. Allison raised her eyebrows in the direction she came from and contemplated what she was going to do.

Apparently, the infamous Daniel somehow tracked her down to ambush her at this ball. That would mean, he must have followed her and found out who she was. She started to panic. It didn't make sense. He left. Why would he track her down, and here?

The pieces didn't fit together. She stared blindly at the shimmering water fall beyond the tables trying to figure out how he found her. It was only one night. They didn't know each other's last names, it was near impossible to figure out who she was, unless he was a crazy stalker, as well as a sexy, gorgeous-- she needed to stop letting her mind carry her away.

The world became too small at that moment. Her stomach growled. She hadn't eaten anything for about six hours now, and her body did not accept that.

Allison glanced towards the buffet table, contemplating whether to try again, or to call it a night and grab a bite to eat at her hotel. She decided. She would eat at the ball. The food looked too good. As she got up from her chair, she noticed Daniel heading towards the table. Allison did not need this right now. He was not going to keep her from her dinner any longer. As she opened her month to say something, her boss, Mr. Osmund rose to meet Daniel.

She was in shock. Her body froze where she stood and her face muscles loosened causing her mouth to hang open. They both glanced over at her, Daniel, and her boss. Every step they took caused Allison to ratchet up the alarm meter. Her boss knowing Daniel, with body language like he was slightly afraid, if not extremely respectful of him made her brain hurt. Her brain literally stopped working. If her body didn't have a self preservation mechanism built it, she would have dropped dead because none of her organs would work. Her brain was on short circuit.

As they walked over to her, Allison raced through as many scenarios as her poor brain could muster. She was left with a black screen with white scrolling writing across the screen and the "this is a test" beep buzzing through her head.

They stopped in front of her. There was no reason for Daniel to disclose their affair was there? He wouldn't. Daniel had a sly smirk on his face, and Mr. Osmund looked excited.

"Ms. Caine, I would like you to meet Mr. Bryson Anderson Jr. You two will be working closely over the next week, and I'm so glad Mr. Anderson is here tonight. We weren't sure if he would show up, but he did." Mr. Osmund gave Bryson a hearty pat on the back, then backed off, alternating between giddy excitement professional composure. Mr. Osmund looked at Allison, his expression betraying the importance he put on Bryson and the money he represented to the firm.

More professionally he said. " That way tomorrow, you two can get right to work."

Daniel, or Bryson, or maybe it was Jimmy Hoffa, who knew? reached out his hand.

"Nice to meet you Ms. Caine, I've heard many wonderful things about you. It's going to be a pleasure working with you over the next few days."

He was laying it on thick, thought Allison. He heard? From who, himself?

Mr. Osmund looked at Allison expectantly. She quickly reached her hand out to Bryson.

"Good to meet you Mr. Anderson." The words felt fake and bitter in her mouth. She didn't sleep with a Mr. Anderson. That wasn't the name that left her lips in ecstasy. This man looked like him, but was an imposter.

That was all Allison could get out. If another syllable left her mouth, she was liable to swear, the likes Mr. Osmund had never heard. She still had the good sense to salvage her career.


Samantha saw the frozen look on her friends face and immediately knew something was wrong. She was momentarily taken aback by the gorgeous man she was shaking hands with, but her concern was for her friend.

She turned to the lady she was sitting next to, Lady Byum, who claimed to know everything about everyone, and inquired on who the sexy man next to Allison was. He had to be the reason she was having a freak out moment.

"Oh Dear. That's Bryson Anderson. I hear he's quite the ladies man. If I was only twenty, who am I kidding thirty years younger, I would knock his socks off."

Samantha wasn't listening. She apologized to the bird looking man next to her after the water she was drinking flew out of her mouth under so much pressure, some had to escape from her nose. In later retelling the story, Samantha would be sure to include how that made her almost drown. When whoever was listening looked at her with skeptical eyes, she would remind them they could drown in a tablespoon of water. But only if you stopped breathing and did not blow said water out of your nose.

Sam put the water down on the table and bolted out of her chair. Her peach chiffon dress snagged on the foot of the table, but she didn't falter. She eased up beside her friend, who for all intensive purposes was frozen solid where she stood.

Mr. Osmund had taken Bryson away to meet more of the company. Alli was left looking like a lone island in the middle of the ocean.

Sam gently placed Allison's hand in hers and squeezed. She gingerly lead Allison away, whispering coaching instructions along the way.

"Walk with me Alli, one step in front of the other. That's good. Just like that."

It continued like that. Whispered encouragements to guide her friend out of the ballroom. She needed to get out of there. Needed fresh air. The large ballroom was starting to feel small and stuffy. Sam lead Alli out of the ballroom to the stairs that lead to the sandy beach behind the Colosseum. Everyone was inside. The women didn't want to mess up their abhorrently expensive dresses, and the men didn't want sand in their shoes. The wind blew their hair all around them. The vast blackness of the sea was overwhelming, but it brought Alli back to reality. Her brain started up again with a rumble.

"Sam, did you hear that? Do you know who that was? Who I was being introduced to a minute ago was?"

Allison stared imploringly into Sam's face.

"Yes Alli, I know."

"I told you it was a conspiracy. They're trying to ruin me." Allison was devastated. She believed herself. "Sam, it was only once. You know me. I've never done that before, ever. It was a mistake Sam, a moment of weakness."

Allison was starting to cry. Her big deep eyes filled with tears faster than Cry Babys' (Johnny Depp!). "Do you realize, my mistake, my one night of indiscretion is standing in that ballroom claiming to be Bryson Anderson Jr.!"

"Not claiming Alli, that is Bryson Anderson Jr." Allison looked at her best friend of over ten years like she was seeing her for the first time.

"No Sam, he can't be. That would mean, the man who showed me the greatest love making of my life after just meeting him, the man who left me in the morning like a two bit whore without knowing his real name, the man whose child is growing inside of me right now, is the same man I have to spend the next week with; Bryson Anderson Jr."

# *THREE*

BRYSON HAD TO CATCH himself from tripping over air, as he made his way outside. His mind scrambled for a second, as he tried to make sense of what he just heard. He looked around him for what almost made him fall on his face, but couldn't find anything physical. It was the shock of hearing that he was going to be a Dad.

"A baby? My baby?" he said to himself.

He saw her go outside and thought it was a great place to talk to her, away from everyone. He didn't know he was walking into an upper cut that would knock him out. He hadn't intended to eavesdrop on Allison and her friend, but he was glad he did....a baby? Bryson was relieved that he whispered that last statement and was far enough away so Allison or her friend could not hear him. He walked across the sand, looking for a place to discreetly sit and listen. He was all into the spying now. The warm night blew soft breezes across his skin. The night ocean air smelled clean and fresh. Sand seeped into his shoes, piling up under his feet as he walked. He finally found a spot behind a large shrub, manually placed there for decoration. He balanced on a large smooth rock and listened. And listened, but he didn't hear them. Instead he heard his heart pounding in his ears and his palms were starting to get clammy. His breathing came fast and heavy and he was about to lose it.

He handled multi million dollar deals on a daily basis. He had hunted with heads of States, had contentious disagreements with very dangerous people, while a tiny little eight pound baby scared him?

Bryson snapped out of it.

*It's a baby, not the end of the world*, he thought. He was unprepared, wasn't ready, and caught of guard. He planned everything, almost everything, and processing a child, his child into existence was terrifying. He figured in three to five years he may start a family, but now, not now.

This was not part of the plan. To have a baby, especially with a woman he barely knew would only spell disaster.

So yeah, the sex was great, mind blowing actually, but what kind of person was she. They may have fit together flawlessly, but that did not constitute a parental relationship. Bryson didn't know if he wanted her to be the mother of his heir.

It started as a smirk and grew into a full smile with teeth and all. His heir. A part of him growing inside Allison. Developing little tiny fingers and toes. Growing arms and legs. Getting a smile and ears and a little button nose with lungs, and a little heart that beat. In a few months the little tyke would be a living breathing person.

It's own person. His person. The responsibility was overwhelming. To be accountable for another life, a small helpless little life, seemed impossible. He could manage and direct hundreds, even thousands of people with no problem, but was unsure if he could be in charge of a baby's life successfully. He tried not to fail at anything.

Maybe it was the vastness of the star filled Caribbean sky, or the few tequila shots he downed at the Ball, or maybe it was a buried yearning peaking it's head from it's hiding place, but Bryson's outlook changed.

Instead of fear and dread of this new life, instead of feeling trapped, he saw the figure of his child materialize in front of him, playing. He saw himself playing catch with his son, or daughter, taking his kid to the Braves games back home, teaching his son how to tie a tie, or carrying his baby girl on his shoulders as they played.

It felt good. It felt right, like something he'd discovered he wanted more and more desperately with every second that passed, and every breath he took.

Life, Bryson thought at that moment, was very colorful. He'd traveled from the mountains of Chile, to the seas of the Mediterranean looking for life. Looking for adventure, whether on the ski slopes or in a woman's bed. The adrenaline of skydiving, or the high from netting large sums of money from his business transactions satisfied him for a moment. But he always felt empty soon after, which led him looking for his next high, his next adventure, his next sale, his next warm bed. But now, he was getting an heir. Life was smiling at him, giving him something he didn't know he wanted, but was just what he needed.

Bryson sat on his rock fantasizing about all the things he would do and all the things he would give to his kid when he heard, " ....give it up for adoption."

It took all of his strength to keep his position on the rock behind the shrubs. He zoned back in to the conversation going on between Allison and her friend. Panic replacing his reverie.

"Are you sure you will be able to do that when the time comes? I mean why not keep the baby?"

It sounded like muffed sobbing through the shrubs before Bryson heard

" ...because for one, I thought about getting an abortion, but I couldn't go through with it, and two, I don't want to be a single mother , I don't want to raise a child by myself. A fatherless child is not what I want for any kid. This child deserves better than I can give it. I can't do it."

"But your child has a father, he's in there right now."

More muffled sobbing was followed by, "he left me Sam. Left me...alone. Why would he want this child. What if he says it's not his, or thinks I purposely got pregnant to get at his money? It's easier this way."

"Don't you think he has a right to know, to have a vote in this decision--"

"He gave up his right when he left me, okay?" Bryson had a mind to jump out from behind the shrubs and lay down the law. Tell her what they were going to do. She would have to quit her job immediately. As the mother of his child, she would need to stay home with their child. She would have to learn the art of entertaining, and how to be on his arm, but that could be taken care of. Plus, he would tell her they were getting married, immediately.

Yes, there would be murmurs, but that was better than Bryson Anderson Jr having an illegitimate child. His reputation may get scuffed, but he wanted to see where this conversation was going.

"Keep your voice down Allison, you don't want anyone to hear you."

"Look, I've already made my decision, before I came here and found out about Bryson. This changes nothing. To me his presence means nothing. I'll do my job, leave this island, and get on with my life. That's all I want is for things to go back to normal."

"Not if I have anything to say about it," whispered Bryson. Allison had his Heir growing within her and he couldn't, wouldn't just let that go.

"No matter what you do Alli, you can't go back to normal," said Allison's friend.

Her friend hit the nail on the head thought Bryson. To have his child be given away, to not know his kid or have any contact with his child was unacceptable. Anger started to seep into his veins. Who did she think she was. Hiding something so important from him. Bryson wasn't an unreasonable man, and he knew he had a part to play in Allison's decision. If he confronted her too harshly, with too many demands, she may run from him and who knows what she would do then. All she'd have to do is hide out until the baby was born before being found again.

He wouldn't let that happen. He wasn't a billionaire because he was stupid. He would have to tread lightly with Allison. He needed her to see it his way, to come to his side. Even if she didn't want to be with him emotionally, they would have to work out an agreement professionally.

He had to figure out a way to convince Allison to not give up their kid for adoption, but to raise it with him, like a partnership. All while not divulging that he'd heard she was pregnant. He needed her to tell him on her own so she wouldn't feel confronted. Let her be in control. The more he thought about it, the better the idea sounded.

# *FOUR*

BEING LANDLOCKED IN ATLANTA, Allison couldn't get use to the ocean everywhere she turned. She was walking to work, the first day of the audit, dressed in her very corporate and conservative grey skirt suit in her heels and attache case looking around, in wonder. She didn't know how any business could get done. Everything seemed so demure, so at ease, like everyone was on vacation all the time. She was only a block away from the ocean where she saw three cruise liners docked. Low colorful buildings lined the streets behind street vendors setting up to market to the revolving tourists due out of their slumber in a few hours. The warm morning sun warmed her skin and gave her a sun-kissed glow. She felt good. Last night was very traumatic for her, but she'd come to terms, not only with what she had to do, but with her decisions about her child. All she needed to do, was to get through one week. One week. Then she would never have to see him again. The thought made her smile.

Before she reached the building, she smelled a few merchants cooking, and it made her mouth water. She had to get in and get some coffee and maybe a bagel. A small chuckle escaped the side of her mouth while she reached for the heavy glass and metal door. Allison was starting to gain an unhealthy obsession with food. She thought about it all the time, and she was only two months pregnant.

A burst of cold air bombarded her, making Allison's nipples wake up and shout to everyone within ten feet, hey everyone, overhear, look at me. Good thing the only person around was a old security guard, more concerned with his monitor than her. He glanced at her and went back to what he was doing.

The cold air brought her into pro mode. Ready to conquer....the audit. Accounting wasn't very exciting, but it paid well enough, and numbers weren't emotional. They didn't have feelings and couldn't hurt her. She always knew what the answer was as long as she worked it out. Everyone knew the rules with numbers and everyone was subject to the same rules. Numbers didn't want and burn for a man that deceived, and used others so casually, and so easily. Numbers didn't hate and love at the same time. They were just numbers, static and unchanging.

To run into Bryson last night after Allison worked so hard in the last couple of months, to come to terms with her abandonment, brought all of her feelings for him back. Anger, lust, pain, arousal, insult, and wanting, all at the same time. She told herself it was because she was pregnant with his baby that she felt such a sexual attraction to Bryson. An attraction so powerful it made her breath catch, if she ever let her guard down. She couldn't allow herself to day-dream, or night dream as it may. Her mind and body confused her to no end.

She'd had enough. Allison was taking control, starting now.

She couldn't wait to finish her audit so she could get on a plane back to Atlanta, and away from this tortuous paradise. She reached the elevators, signaled for one, and waited. Her heels tapped impatiently on the marble floors, as she glanced at her watch.

Allison was early, really early. She'd arrived two hours before she was scheduled to come in. She wanted to settle in, figure out her surroundings, and get a feel for the place.

Allison waited for the elevator, not paying much attention to her surroundings.

"I didn't expect to see you here so early," said a deep musical voice.

Startled, Allison jumped to attention and came face to face with the one person who could speed up her heart rate.

"Mr. Anderson, good morning." She pasted a plastered smile that made her look like if her smile went any further, she would shatter into a million pieces.

*Do not let him get to me, do not let him get to me,* repeated Allison over and over in her head.

Bryson paused before he answered. A slow smirk appeared on his face.

"Allison, I think we are beyond such formalities. Mr. Anderson? I prefer you call me Bryson."

He slowly took in Allison. His eyes moved from her cute black pumps to, her smooth shapely legs. He remembered them wrapped around his neck and wanted them there again, but he needed something else from her.

Her gray form fitting dress started below the knee, but all that did was highlight her curvy hips and round substantial ass. His eyes trailed her stomach and reached her nipples which called out for him to suck on them, now. He sucked in a breath and settled on her heart shaped face. Her hair was pulled back into a sensible bun, but he knew of the wild thick curls Allison was holding in. The ding of the elevator arriving brought Bryson out of his trance.

"After you, Allison."

"No, you go on, I'll wait for the next one."

"The elevator is big enough for the both of us. What...? Are you scared to be in the same place as me?" Bryson was amused. She really was going to try and avoid him. It was his company and she was working for him, he wondered how she planned to do that.

"Scared...huh... hardly, I decided it is best that we keep our distance from each other over the next few days," replied Allison.

"Look, the elevator is already here, we are going to the same floor, it doesn't make sense that we take separate elevators. We're both adults. Besides, I'll only bite if you want me to," said Bryson with a wicked smirk on his face.

"Oh Please..fine lets go."

"After you Allison."

"No, After you Bryson." Allison didn't need any hospitality from him, she knew who he was and he wasn't going to fool her again. Plus, she didn't want him starring at her ass as she walked by.

"Suit yourself."

Bryson stepped into the elevator followed by Allison. The doors closed and Allison felt like she was in a sauna although the building's air conditioning was set at sixty five degrees. They were only going to the fifth floor. It seemed no buildings in the Cayman Islands were higher than five stories, but the elevator was moving slower than a turtle. She was almost there.

"So what is this about avoiding me for the next few days?" Bryson turned to look at Allison, but Allison kept her eyes ahead of her as she watched the numbers on the elevator slowly advance. She didn't speak. Her neck tilted slightly away from Bryson and he could hear her let out an aggravated breath. Allison hated being in such a small space with him. She could feel him next to her, smell him next to her, a mix of cinnamon and summer. It was sweet and husky at the same time. He smelled good, too good.

His smell activated her libido, and her wrath, simultaneously. Maybe she could get him to back off. She put as much venom as she could muster in her eyes and voice and replied, "What do you want from me? Actually you got what you wanted already so don't answer that. I mean..what are you doing? Are you trying to make conversation? Why?"

It was Bryson's turn to get aggravated. He didn't like to be ignored and brushed off like a fly on a sandwich. No one disregarded him, or treated him with anything less than the utmost respect. He didn't like it one bit. Bryson reached for Allison's arm and turned her towards him.

"I don't need your attitude. Obviously, I'm trying to talk to you because we have some unresolved issues to contend with-"

"Unresolved issues? Listen buddy," said Allison, as she poked her right index finger into his hard chest. "Any issues that may have needed to be resolved, consider them resolved. I have nothing more to discuss with you, I have not-thing..." a poke of her finger to Bryson's chest to articulate every syllable ..."to re-solve with you...you... you......asshole!"

Without realizing it, Allison had tensed up with her hands at her sides balled up in a fist, trembling slightly. She was heaving with daggers in her eyes as she stared at him. It felt like over a hundred degrees in the elevator at that moment. Water started to form on Bryson's temples as he started back at Allison. She knew all the right buttons to press to incense him.

"Ass--"

Ding! The elevator reached the fifth floor and the doors opened. Allison turned, shrugged herself out of his grasp and walked out of the elevator. But she didn't know where to go. She walked a few steps then turned around to ask Bryson how to get to her office, but he was gone.

"Good, I don't need you anyway." She whispered under her breath and headed towards the end of the hallway to search for her temporary office, while mentally counting down the days to get rid of her temporary problem.

"I don't need anyone."

Before Allison reached the office she was assigned, she had to find the bathroom. She'd come in early so she wouldn't be flustered, running around franticly, trying to find her way. Yet, here she was doing just that. She figured the bathrooms were either at the ends of the hallway or exactly in the middle. The carpet made her footsteps silent, but anyone who saw Allison could see her distress. Mascara made a path down her cheeks. Her eyes, usually bright and alert were red and cloudy. Allison sped up as she saw the bathroom closing in. Never having been there before, Allison hoped the bathroom wasn't one of those communal bathrooms with stalls. She wanted the privacy of getting herself together without anyone else walking in or out.

When she pushed the door open, Allison gasped, shocked at what she saw. A double sink granite countertop with marble floor lined the wall. A be-day and toilet sat in a room by itself and the mirror was massive. *Wow*, Allison thought, they live well here at Anderson Properties. At the thought of Bryson's name and company, Allison huffed and walked into the bathroom. If just the sight of the bathroom and the thought of his name got Allison in a fit, how did she feel she would get through the rest of the week?

The next few days were going to be torture and Allison knew it. Pure and simple, nails on the blackboard, water-boarding, torture. The quickness to anger and the freak out episodes were starting to grate on Allison's nerves. Realization hit her on the head. She was acting like a baby. A spoiled little baby. Ironic, considering she was pregnant.

At her desk, the numbers flowed into one. Three hundred thousand, five hundred and fifty eight dollars and twenty three cents, melded into two thousand four hundred dollars even. She couldn't concentrate, and that was unacceptable. Over her shoulder, her co-worker Andrew was staring at her, looking, preying for anything that was off. She could feel it. He wanted her job, and he was the type to do anything to get it. No one at the firm knew how he'd meddle his way into the trip. He was barely there six months. His hot breath made Allison want to barf. It smelled like twice eaten tuna fish. She looked at him ready to offer him some tic-tacs she found in her bag, and noticed something stuck in his teeth. She looked away trying to keep her lunch down.

"So what ya working on there Ally McBeal." That was another thing. He made everyone in the office call her Ally McBeal. It didn't even make any sense to her. He was just lazy, he heard her name was Allison, and that was the first thing the simple guy made up.

"The audit. Shouldn't you be working instead of leaning over me?" she replied. *Breathing your hot stinky breath on my neck*, she thought to herself. If her hair wasn't already curly, it would have surely curled up now.

"I'm making sure you are doing it right."

She thanked God she didn't have an ice pick handy because she really felt like jabbing it into his head. Doing it right? Andrew had an uncanny way to say simple things that grated under her skin.

"Andrew, I'm not in the mood. Please move back and let me get back to what I'm doing." With a deep breath she turned back to her computer and battled with all the numbers that once again started to meld together.

"I'm just giving you a heads up. I heard Mr. Osmund doesn't think you care about the opportunities he's given you, he thinks you've lost your sense of focus. I know this audit is kinda a make or break for you. If you f this up, that's your ass." Andrew had a very satisfied look on his face as he finished his unwanted "heads up".

"At the CEO's ball, he introduced me to everyone and he had no complaints. Didn't you—that's right, you weren't invited. Sorry about that. You should have been there it was amaaazing. You really should have been there. Maybe you'll get invited next time."

Allison knew what she was doing. She knew Andrew wanted to go and was shut out. She may have zinged Andrew but it didn't negate what he said.

She may not have heard Mr. Osmund say it, but she felt it was true. She'd been late lately, missing work due to morning sickness and doctors appointments. At work she was distant and out of it, and she knew everyone noticed.

At a time when her boss was trying to catapult the firm into the upper echelons of Atlanta businesses, her performance was no good. She even almost lost a client when she totally F up his monthly report, and made it seem like he owed fifty thousand dollars more in taxes than he actually did. If it wasn't for her great relationship with her boss and some heavy making up to the client, the firm wouldn't have been able to retain the client. The client still looks at her funny whenever they run into each other.

"I'm just trying to help," he continued a little wounded but determined. If Alli get's canned, he moves into her spot. She was the one thing standing in his way of his five year plan. Get Allison out of the way and be one step closer to management.

"Thanks for your concern Andrew, but I am fully capable and able to handle my duties." Why did he pick now to mess with her, to put such doubts and innuendo in her head. She'd had a terrible morning. Her stomach was starting to growl, she didn't know if she was hungry or not because she'd just eaten a bagel. She had no time or inclination to battle with Andrew. The father of her baby was a few hundred feet from her, in his big office, feeling like he owned the world, and she was battling with a dip twit co worker out for her neck.

Alli tapped her heels on the corporate dark grey carpet to steady her nerves. She felt good that it made no noise.

She would hate for Andrew, "Andy Dick" as he was called around the office behind his back, to notice she was bothered.

"Alright, I'm just saying."

He rolled his chair back to his desk and started to play solitaire. That's all he did all day, play computer games, social networking, and scheme. He did just enough work not to get fired, but he used his interpersonal skills with the bosses to gain influence.

Andrew could plan all he wanted, Allison was here to stay. She wouldn't and couldn't let either Bryson Anderson Jr., Andrew, or the baby growing inside of her, throw off her plans. She wouldn't let Bryson or Andrew win.

It was decided.

She would work her ass off and hopefully minimize the damage to her career that this baby would do. As soon as she got back to Atlanta, she would start to search for a family for her baby.

It sounded good, but what Allison wouldn't admit to herself was the life developing in her was starting to grow on her. She didn't know if she could do the things that according to her, solved all her problems.

As the numbers started to regain their places on her spreadsheet, she hoped it was as easy as she'd just imagined it to be. Allison didn't think it would be, but she'd cross that bridge when she got to it. For now, she just had to avoid Bryson for the next four days, and try to go back to her life. She wondered if the saying, you can never go back home, would apply to her. Would all that she'd experienced in the Caymans alter anything? She didn't know and now was a terrible time to think about it. She had work to do.

# *FIVE*

"ASSHOLE? THE NERVE OF HER!" Bryson was furious. Once again, Allison had the audacity to call him, names? She was the one keeping his child a secret. How dare she treat him this way?

He passed the rows of gray cubicles without seeing them, and slammed his office door behind him. Bryson punched his hard wooden desk, and let out a sound, almost a grunt, but closer to an aggravated sigh. If the floors in his office were carpeted, track marks where he always paced when he was upset, would be visible. The terracotta floors only showed a little wear, on his usual pacing route.

Everything was getting out of hand. This was not part of his plan. He figured he would be able to have a civil conversation with Allison and somehow work out the mess they were in, to a satisfactory arrangement. Another grunt came from Bryson. Mess? Accidently shattering a plate is a mess, this was a catastrophe.

There were no MBA programs, no mentor he could go to for advice on how to seduce the mother of his baby. Throw in hurt feelings, a pregnancy coverup, mix and bake for two and a half months, and attempt to gain a family. Wow, it sounded crazy, even to him.

The difficulty level went up ten fold because Allison was carrying so much animosity towards him. That caught him totally by surprise. That changed everything. There was no talking any sense into her. This was his Heir after all. If anything was worth saving, it would be this. There were no guarantees he would be able to intercept the adoption or even adopt his own child when the time came, if it came to that. There were too many variables and room for failure.

Bryson planned not to fail. Anything he did, needed to have a very high probability of success, or there was no use in doing them. That was his theory, but things didn't always work out the way they were planned. He leaned back in his leather chair and stared at the turquoise ocean out of his floor to ceiling windows.

Tourists were starting to disembark from the cruise line boats docked just outside his building. From where he sat, the colorful people in their bright yellows and reds, looked like miniature people wandering along the street, not knowing where to go or what to do. All the people he watched, he knew, needed guidance. Someone to tell them the best place to eat, the best shops to buy souvenirs, and the places to avoid.

No one had to tell him what to do the first time he had the pleasure of meeting Allison. His mind took him back to that beautiful day in Atlanta. The weather was beautiful, but cold. He felt cold inside and out. The Paramount Condo project wasn't doing well and he needed to unload as many units as he could, before the proverbial bottom fell out. The writing was on the wall, sell now, or be stuck with two hundred Condo units sitting and collecting dust, and earning him nothing, while costing him millions in maintenance.

The fire-sale was a colleagues idea. Sell the units below value, and in some instances below cost, just to cut his loses. That was the wind that blew Allison into his life.

She looked beautiful in a girl next door way. Tussled hair flying around and framing her face with a glowing smile from cheek to cheek. Her vibe said happy, open, and sweet.

And smart. She must have grabbed up a Condo or was about to. The look she had on her face said she'd won something. Her win probably cost him tens of thousands of dollars. Her gait was elegant, and her body curvy and voluptuous.

She looked hot. Bryson knew the warmth of countless women worldwide, but Allison awakened a primal need he didn't know he had.

She may be a hothead, but she was a fine hothead. His body recognized and wanted her immediately. Allison walked into his life like a tornado. Humming with laughter in her eyes and a smile that captured his body, mind, and soul.

There to take advantage of the deals, she walked into the Condo Bryson was evaluating before he left town. His standards were high. Although he was selling the units off at unbelievably low prices, it was still his building.

Therefore, the units had to convey the quality and luxury of an Anderson property.

Giggling, Allison and her friend ran from room to room commenting on how they were going to decorate. Where they were going to put what, and what a great price they got. Her voice was harmonic, lyrical.

Before they saw him, her friend received a phone call and had to leave.

He'd heard it all, staying quiet and enjoying the happiness of the girls. At least someone was happy.

The apartment was large. With three bedrooms and three and a half bathrooms, the girls were able to explore without noticing him in the living room. The metal door of the condo slammed shut, and when Allison turned around and saw him, she drew in a surprised breath and covered her mouth with her hands.

"Oh my God, I didn't know anyone else was here. The receptionist downstairs said this condo was empty. I am so sorry." He didn't have sales reps selling the condos. The plan allowed those who signed in to explore the condos at will and return to the main office to purchase the one they wanted.

Bryson was tickled by her apology. He didn't understand why she was apologizing. She seemed the type though. If someone bumped into her, she would be the one to apologize. Her large eyes were so dark they seemed black, but bright and concerned at the same time. The sound of her voice was melodic and soothing. Not too high with a nice rosy undertone. He wanted to hear her voice again.

"You know you did disturb me. Here I am minding my own business and I get bombarded in on," said Bryson.

"You must understand, I didn't know anyone was here. I'll be gone soon," replied Allison. She was tapping her fingers against her legs, betraying how embarrassed she really was.

Bryson became more intrigued. Her nervousness made him want to soothe her, protect her from any and everything that would embarrass or make her nervous.

"I'm sorry you can't leave, you still have to make it up to me," said Bryson.

His face was as stoic as any Judge passing down a judgement. She raised one eyebrow, a skill he thought amazing, bit her lip and stared at him.

"Seriously?" asked Allison. She saw the flicker of a smirk cross his face before he was able to correct it. She relaxed and smiled easily with him.

"You had me there for a minute."

She let out a soft laugh. She was cute when she laughed. She had a sexy way of biting her lip when she was unsure of herself. The act ignited Bryson's libido which lately was out on vacation. No one made his blood rush faster through his veins, his heart beat stronger, and no one got him harder than steel.

Until her.

And he didn't even know her name.

"I would like to have you for more than a minute." Bryson watched as Allison tensed up. He hoped he didn't scare her off. He was never one for subterfuge and innuendo but, he may have to back off her just a little.

"I uh....uh, are you kidding again?" delivered with a smile, a reluctant smile because Allison's cheeks got red. But she didn't turn and run out of the apartment screaming either. She stood her ground eyebrows knitted trying to figure him out.

"Hi, friends call me Daniel, you are?" He walked over to Allison and extended his hand. She took it. Her hands were soft and delicate that hid a firm handshake.

He considered giving his real name, but Bryson Anderson Jr was a very powerful and public name. His family owned a substantial portion of the condos in Atlanta, and commercial shopping centers being built in the suburbs. This girl obviously didn't know who he was, or how much money he had. They were there as two people talking and flirting with each other, and it felt good.

For Bryson, he had such a recognizable last name, anonymity was a luxury he didn't often experience.

"I'm Allison, I Didn't know we were friends?"

"Que Sera Sera," said Bryson waving his hand dismissively.

"So, my new friend Daniel, what are you doing here? The receptionist didn't say anything about anyone being here. Oh,..please don't tell me you're thinking about buying THIS unit?"

"Oh no, I own this entire condo building and when you own things, you can do what you want with them." He gave her his stone serious face again.

"HA, you wish, and I'm the Queen of England." Her hands went to her hips then highlighting the dark blue denim hugging her curvy hips. The red turtle neck accentuated her breasts perfectly and her nipples were trying to make an appearance. Distracted, Bryson realized she didn't believe him. He missed a few words before tuning back in when she said.,

"...Sam and I, we really like this place and it would be perfect for us, the price is just what we can afford, plus look at this view." She walked over to the floor to ceiling glass wall spreading her arms in order to capture the expansive view, as she peered out at the Atlanta skyline.

"Look at this view. It's absolutely perfect."

Bryson was concentrating on another view. Allison's derriere was calling to him. His pants moved slightly at the thought of having her on the couch right now in front of the beautiful view. The view was excellent. He walked up beside Allison and felt her hold her breath, but he didn't feel fear coming from her. That would totally ruin the mood and any chance he had of knowing any more of this beautiful, sexy girl.

He'd already decided. He wanted to know more about Allison. He wanted to know if she bit her lips during sex like she did when she was bothered. He wanted to hear how his name sounded on her lips as he brought her to climax again and again.

She turned to face him, moving as if in slow motion, averting her eyes until the last possible moment.

They locked eyes. His black hair was wavy and cropped close to his head. The air around them became charged with a force that had both of them breathing a little heavier than needed.

He wanted her.

Badly.

His body was vibrating with a primal urge to claim, but his modern brain just wanted to party. He jumped back and forth, his erection existing regardless of his primal or modern need. Her heavy breathing made him feel she was going through the same dilemma either way, he wanted her with him.

But, would she go?

Bryson cut the sexual energy flowing through the condo with his right hand as he placed it on her shoulder.

The contact created a buzz of electricity throughout his body. Allison swayed a little and closed her eyes. She must have felt it too. He watched her, trying to determine if she was down or not. Another buzz roared through his body, causing his head to cloud with overwhelming lust. Allison moaned, and he knew he wasn't the only one experiencing the strange but exciting sensations.

"You want to get out of here and go get something to eat?"

"Like what?" Asked Allison with a sly smile.

It took all the years of Bryson's practiced training in negotiations not to break down and throw Allison on the nearby couch and make a meal of her until she trembled, spent and motionless.

She was teasing him. Softly one minute, unsure of herself, direct the next, willing him to play with her.

"Let's go up the block to the hotel restaurants and see what they have available?"

He reached for her hand and waited while she decided what she was going to do. If she didn't come with him, he would leave depressed and dejected. Allison brought out such intense sensations, he didn't know how to handle it if she denied him. Sweat formed at his temples and his nerves rattled uncontrollably. He was in a position he hated to be in, but for Allison, he would endure the torture of her assessment.

She stared from Bryson's outstretched hands to his golden eyes and back again. Looking for what, he didn't know. The quiet was deafening He was about to drop his hands when she raised her hand to lock with his.

A satisfied smile lit his face and a sexy, welcoming smile lit hers.

That's when he knew, she wanted to know more about him too.

Back in his office, a smile sneaked it's way onto Bryson's face. The easy exchanges he had with Allison, the softness of her smiles, and company was a refreshing change, to the marriage ambitious women he usually dated. The last woman he dated, Jessica, spent their entire first date talking about this and that designer and who among her friends just got married with what carat diamond ring.

The sex at the end of the date was good, but it wasn't enough. Jessica had a great way of putting herself together, and they looked like a great couple but had nothing in common. They say opposites attract, but not that time.

Now, there was a big push to get him married and soon. The person his advisors and parents preferred was nice enough, and a good friend, but didn't ignite the passion in him that Allison did.

Allison, she was something all together different. From the beginning they were able to comfortably have fun. The memories of when they met made him smile.

*She wasn't so bad.* From their first meeting they were able to laugh, relax and be free together. It felt good not having to be on high alert constantly wondering if the person he's with wanted anything from him other than a good time.

It felt good taking a break from the fight, and strategy of the business world. It felt good to go out like two normal people without all the baggage of the Anderson name.

Bryson was content to have a show wife, a wife for the public while he fought and worked for wealth and status. However, after meeting and spending time with Allison, she ignited a primal fire that burned hot and deep, that desired more than money, or status. He wanted love, adoration, fun...a family.

The shock of Allison's pregnancy, the knowledge of a little Bryson growing inside of her was great news.

If only she felt the same way. This was his chance. Maybe they wouldn't have undying and intense love, but they were two people that could have fun together, two people that could develop a mutual partnership, and get along great. Partnerships he could do, personal relationships, that was a different story.

Resolved to get Allison on his side, he plotted a way to get through to her. He reached for his phone and buzzed his secretary.

"Saundra, schedule a meeting between the auditor Allison Caine for seven P.M tonight and tell her it's from a Mr. Osmund."

"Yes sir, Mr. Anderson right away."

He hung up the phone with a renewed sense of hope. This will work, it had to.

Deval "Sean" Patel brought the shot glass of whiskey to his lips trying as hard as he could to control his trembling hands. After the sixth shot, the whiskey no longer burned his lips, but still stung a little as he gulped the warm liquid down his throat. Pretty soon, it would be all Sean had, his whiskey and his shot glass. He slammed his glass down on the solid mahogany end table and rolled back into bed.

Although it was almost noon, Sean's bedroom felt like the middle of the night. He'd installed heavy drapes to block out the light of the day when he found that the sun annoyed him. He was a night owl, all his business, he would rather do at night, under the cover of darkness.

Sean slept under burgundy twelve hundred count sheets and a three foot skylight, he had covered during the day. The dark marble floors stretched all the way to the fireplace and sitting area. Although he was in the Cayman Islands where the temperature didn't get low enough for a fireplace, Sean felt it showed his wealth, that he could have a totally unnecessary, and expensive object in his bedroom, that would never be used.

Sean didn't notice the feather soft sheets, nor did he see the Luis Franco Marquis painting he'd paid a small fortune for, hanging in the southeast corner of the room. Instead, he kept trying to figure out how to stop Bryson Anderson Jr. from taking over his family's hotel.

As the youngest Patel of the Patel clan, it took Sean a considerable amount of positioning, time and scheming, plus the death of his father to become the CEO of Sunsplash resorts. It was all going so well. Sean was thirty two when his father Mushar Patel had died suddenly and left Sean, not his older brother Punjay "Patrick" Patel head of all companies and assets.

It was all over the papers, and Sean was considered one of the most eligible bachelors. Young, good looking with his midnight black hair that always fell over his right eye, and dark commanding eyes with a touch of navy in the corners, left women around the world in awe. Sean had a smile that could dazzle the panties off any girl, and a body that he loved to show off, running along the beaches in the South of France.

Sean had it all, and like many people who don't earn their fortune, he let his wealth and fame get the best of him. After Sean's father's sudden death, his mother was close behind. Within three weeks, Sean and his brother were on their own. With Sean being the main beneficiary of the Patel family's assets, Patrick his brother had to make a choice. Either, live under the shadow and thumb of his younger brother or go out in the world and make it on his own. After all, the Patel name was widely known and respected around the world.

Patrick choose the former and became his younger brothers footstool. That was fifteen years ago. Sean reached for the whiskey bottle again and poured himself another shot. Some of the whiskey spilled onto the side table before he finished pouring. With a soft curse, Sean sat up in bed and started rubbing his bloodshot eyes. He hadn't been able to sleep for the last few days. He was up all night with muscle pain from not moving, and a sick stomach from too much drinking, Sean knew only one thing.

He refused to be poor.

He refused to actually work for a living. Working was for suckers, and Sean was no sucker. But this takeover of Sun-splash would leave him poor if he let it go through as planned.

The women and partying, the Yachts and Estates, the gambling and drinking cost mucho dinero and over time, as he took out more than he was bringing in, Sean became financially upside down, and that's when the borrowing started.

Sean would rather borrow than let anyone know that he was broke. Through all of the scheming to become the

CEO of a big and successful corporation, Sean never considered what it would take to run a successful business.

He figured the money would never stop flowing and things would always be wonderful, because he was rich.

The twenty million dollar investment with Bernie Madoff was the straw that broke the camel's back. In a complex financial deal, Sean put up the resort as collateral against a loan through Bernie's company that Sean didn't even understand. All he knew was he had no more than two weeks before the SEC figured out the paperwork of the loan, and try to take are his family's resort as part of the Madoff investigation.

That's the angle Bryson bullied himself in with. He would buy the resort for an obscenely low amount versus what it was worth and pay Sean five million dollars as parting cash. The SEC and Feds wouldn't get the property and Sean wouldn't be left with nothing. He'd jumped at the deal after Bryson threw in an offer he couldn't refuse.

At first he was satisfied with the five million. He figured he could make a living on five million, but that was before he remembered the money he owed to the Mariachi family out of Italy.

Sean went out and found another buyer. A buyer that would net him ten times the amount Bryson offered. But he was too late, they'd already gone to a tentative contract and the Board of Directors already voted for it. He couldn't get out of the deal, without everyone finding out about his gambling and dealings with Madoff. He needed Bryson to cancel the sale on his own accord.

## *SIX*

SHE ALMOST MADE a clean get-a-way. Allison was opening the cab door when a lady, impeccably dressed in a yellow skirt suit ran out and called to her.

"Ms. Caine, Ms. Caine. I've been trying to reach you ."

"I was just leaving. Is something wrong?"

Out of breath, the lady said, "Oh, I'm Claudia, a Mr. Osmund requests a meeting with you in about two hours at Pappagallo Restaurant, and I needed to let you know."

That immediately made Allison worry. A meeting with her boss couldn't be good right now.

"Is anyone else going to be there?"

"I don't know, I only give the messages."

She handed Allison a post card size note with the address and time of the meeting. She looked at her watch. She only had two hours before she needed to be there. Just enough time to get back to her hotel, change her clothes, relax a bit, then head out.

She didn't want to think about the reasons her boss wanted to meet with her.

Maybe she was getting the axe.

Did she mess anything up at work today? Did that twit Andrew tell him something? Anything Andrew said would be a lie, and she needed to be prepared in case he did say something.

By the time the cab pulled up to the restaurant, Allison's nerves were in tangles. She just knew she would be on a plane by tomorrow, back home to Atlanta, as an utter failure.

She didn't notice how beautiful the restaurant was because she was busy worrying about the viability of her career, the little one growing in her, and her dust up with said little one's father.

It amazed her how she could go from being bored out of her skull, with the highlight of her week watching ER, to her current entanglements.

Only four more days and then she would be back home. Her parents were planning a trip to Atlanta from their home in New York to visit, and she needed to prepare for them. No way could she let them know she was expecting. She wasn't paying attention and screamed when she was greeted by a African gray parrot.

"Ahh Welcome to Pappagallo, Ahh welcome to Pappagallo." said the parrot.

Allison didn't know how to answer a parrot so she just stared. She knew she was frazzled, but determined to make it through the day.

It was almost over.

That is, if she could only keep her mind from jumping from one impossible problem to another. She just stared at the parrot, transfixed.

"Don't mind him, that's only Humphrey Bogart. Do you have a reservation?" said with such nonchalance, it seemed an everyday occurrence.

"Your parrot's name is Humphrey Bogart?"

The server shrugged. "Yeah, he's been here forever."

*Sure*, thought Allison *I'm about to get fired and here I am talking to a parrot.*

"I'm here to meet Mr. Osmund."

The server checked the computer then led Allison to her table.

She wore a a sensible black spaghetti strap dress with a silver cardigan, flat ballerina shoes and a silver purse to dinner.

Pappagallo was a five star restaurant so she wanted to make sure she'd fit into to the ambiance but not stand out. Her makeup was done lightly, with soft pink blush and lip gloss. She couldn't take the smell of any perfume, so her Nivea lotion would have to do.

The restaurant was beautiful, elegant and tropical at the same time. Gold walls greeted Allison as she was escorted through the restaurant to a section separate from everyone else. Soft candles lit the tables and the lighting was so high above her head, she didn't want to bend her head that far back to check them out. The server pulled out her chair when they came to her table for her to sit. Even the chairs were comfortable.

A rose candle burned in a candle holder that muted the soft light. A white table cloth covered the table with a bottle of Cabernet Sauvignon and two glasses. It felt great to slip into the seat and relax. Why Mr. Osmund would have a bottle of wine for her, she didn't know, but she couldn't drink it anyway. She saw a small button on the table—that said press me for service—she pressed in and within a few seconds a waiter arrived at her table.

"Hello, I'm Marcus, How may I help you?"

"Hi Marcus, I would like some cranberry juice please."

"Right away."

A few minutes later, Marcus brought a glass of cranberry juice to her table. The coldness of the cranberry juice created perspiration on the outside of the glass. Allison found herself staring at a drop of water as it made it's way down the glass and onto the white table cloth. Turning her head from side to side, she started to massage her neck. After her meeting with Bryson in the elevator earlier, she felt a pain in her neck that wouldn't go away. She'd been holding her neck tensely all day. The stress of her situation was starting to affect her, physically.

She wouldn't let him cause her physical distress. That had done it. The pain in her neck whenever she thought about Bryson, made her realize she was putting too much into it all. It was time to move on, let go of her anger before it killed her or affected her child negatively.

Allison was no longer living for herself, she was carrying a life. Although she wasn't going to keep the child, she wanted to make sure he or she got a healthy start.

Allison went back to massaging the weight of the day from her neck. She started to fall into the flow of her relaxation when she heard an unmistakably masculine voice.

"Would you like me to help you with that?"

Startled, Allison jumped up in her seat and came face to face with her pain in the neck. Bryson.

"Hello Mr. Anderson, running into you when I don't want to is starting to get old. I'm sorry but I'm unable to spar with you, I'm waiting for someone, so can you please leave?"

It took everything for Allison's voice to be calm and even. Bryson smelled of aftershave, cinnamon and apples with an earthy undertone. His face was smooth where hair should be, His eyes golden and piercing stared at Allison with what Allison thought was a look of amusement. The navy blue golf shirt he wore looked half cotton and half silk. The color made his skin tone shine. His sleeves hugged his muscular arms which reminded Allison of how it felt to be suspended and engulfed in them. The sensation of her hair being pulled firmly but gently as she exploded into ecstasy started a tightening of her stomach and made warm liquid rush throughout her body. She really needed to get a hold of herself whenever she was around Bryson.

"Would you be waiting for Mr. Osmund?" Allison froze.

"He won't be able to make it."

Allison hesitated for just a second before she picked up her purse to leave. The farther away from him she was, the better able she was to keep her resolve.

She placed her left foot out to get out of her chair, but Bryson moved in her way before she could get her right foot to meet her left. During the exchange, Allison's dress retreated a few inches above her knee, and her inner thigh rubbed against Bryson's thigh.

The pressure of his muscular thigh against Allison's core made her head spin. She gasped in a breath and looked up to meet his eyes.

"Where are you going so fast? I just got here." As much as Bryson tried to hide it, his voice caught and Allison felt him harden at their contact.

Desire showed on Bryson's face as clear as saran wrap.

"Can you please move?"

"No." The continued contact between them was getting unbearable. Her panties were getting wet and sooner or later if they stayed this way, Bryson would find out which would probably give him more confidence.

Bryson's arousal gave her a sense of satisfaction. At least she was not the only one affected by their contact.

"We need to talk and I'm not taking no for an answer."

Allison considered insisting to leave. She didn't have to stay, but she would be lying to herself if she said she wasn't a little curious.

"If I stay and listen to you, will you leave me alone."

"You have to hear what I have to say first. If you don't want anything else to do with me, I'll just have to deal with it."

"Fine, move back so I can fix my dress."

"What if I like you like this?"

The daggers flying from her eyes toward Bryson, had him backing up and landed him in a seat across from her.

When the server came, he ordered a beer, and a ribeye steak with mashed potatoes.

"What can I get you?" asked the waiter looking at Allison.

Allison, although curious, wanted to get the meeting over as fast as possible so she declined anything to eat.

"Just some more cranberry juice please."

Bryson jumped in before the Waiter left and said, "I hear the Steak or Pasta dishes here are fantastic. Why don't you try one."

Allison studied Bryson. *Maybe he just wants to prolong the dinner, thought she thought.* But he had a truly concerned look on his face as he made his suggestions. She was a little hungry.

"I won't say anything until after I eat, so you could either sit there and watch me eat, or you could join me."

Allison stubbornly considered sitting there and waiting until he ate. He was blackmailing her with food. She had a mind to take him up on his offer, just not to make him win, but her stomach rebelled and growled at that instant. She scanned the menu.

"I'll have the Lobster Ravioli along with my cranberry juice, thank you."

The waiter left, and they were left alone with each other.

Neither one said a word.

Bryson sat across from her looking confident and sexy. He tried to look her in the eye, but she avoided him. He tried to start small talk, but it went nowhere. They waited for their food, staring out a the gorgeous ocean a few feet from them. The table Bryson reserved for them sat on a balcony a few feet into the ocean. The water lapped up on shore beneath them. The romantic atmosphere was not lost on Allison, and she wished she really was at a romantic dinner, instead of sitting across from a rival.

The Lobster Ravioli was great. It left Allison feeling full and comfortable. After the table was cleared Bryson got down to business.

"I think we got off on the wrong foot," said Bryson.

"You think?"

"Let's push the reset button on us."

"There is no us."

"Well there could be if you give us a chance."

"Why should I? So you could drop me like a sack of bricks, alone and preg- ..and um..alone and preoccupied with you? No thanks...Is that all?"

"No, it's not all." He seemed annoyed.

*Checkmate* thought Allison. She said she would stay and listen, she never agreed to be cordial or agreeable.

"Don't you want to know why?" asked Bryson.

Did she! But Allison didn't know if she really wanted to know the answer.

"I was watching the news the other day. It was about a woman who accidently lost control of her car and slammed head first into a family of four going to Church. The wife, and two kids were killed instantly. The Husband wakes up from a coma after a few days and finds out his entire family is dead. Dead, gone, never to be seen again. Now, does he care why that woman did what she did? Do you think it matters that she was going through a divorce or any thing? Sometimes Bryson the why doesn't matter, just what is. And what is, is we were having a great time, and you left me like a common whore in the morning. That is not who I am and it doesn't matter why. Just that you did what you did," said Allison.

Allison's cheek was heaving in and out and sweat started forming above her lips and forehead.

"Are you saying I'm dead to you?"

Blowing out a puff of air, Allison looked at Bryson incredulously.

"I wasn't talking about you specifically. That was only an example. Look it's getting late and I need my rest."

"Yes you do."

Allison looked up at Bryson, a little curious. Something was off, but she brushed it aside. She reached for her purse and got out of the chair.

"Let me drive you back to your hotel?"

"I'll be fine. I took a cab. I've had enough of your generosity for the evening. Goodbye and thank you for dinner. It was excellent by the way."

Allison turned to go when Bryson reached for her arm and tugged her towards him. Braced against his chest, Allison could smell his cologne. Rough but sweet. She rose to meet his eyes and saw a determination that she didn't know what to do with.

"If you need anything at all Allison, let me know. I mean anything."

Bryson licked his lips.

Momentarily she wanted to soothe the pain she saw in his eyes, but she was hurting too and needed to leave his presence.

Allison turned and left without another word. She had to get away from him, and fast. The response that Bryson induced in her, made her cringe. On one hand she was angry with him, angry that she allowed him to treat her like he did. On the other hand, she still liked him and his body called out to her like a magnet. She was angry with herself that she didn't hate him.

Well, he didn't have to know that.

As she reached the door, she felt a familiar hand on her shoulder. Bryson. What else could he possibly want. Everything was made quite clear.

"What?"

"That is no way to speak to your boss Ms. Caine."

*Oh, so he was going to pull rank.*

"You are not my boss, Mr. Ormund is my boss. You are one of my deceiving clients. I thought with the best education money can buy you'd be able to tell the difference."

"For this job I am your boss and I will remind you if no one else will. Do not speak to me that way. I don't have the time or the inclination to teach you respect that your parents failed to teach you but know this, I will not be your punching bag. If you have anything to say to me that you feel is important, that you feel is making you behave like you don't have any sense, spit it out."

Allison was frozen. Her faced contorted in horror, disbelief, and anger. Tears started welling up deep within her. Before they fell from her eyes, she bit her bottom lip and the tears retreated. With as much control as she could muster Allison replied through clenched teeth.

"After you've disrespected me you speak to ME like this? You have some nerve. I do have something to tell you. I hate you! You have ruined my life and if I could help it I wouldn't see you ever again. You've turned out worse than I thought you were. These next four days can't come and go fast enough."

If Allison wasn't so furious, she would have seen how her words were like cuts, stabs to Bryson. Every syllable causing tiny fissures in him.

"Be that as it may you are required to be at the Roberts Airport at eight a.m in the morning. We have to fly to the Little Island so you can certify some legal documents. These documents don't leave the island so you will need to work with them there. I will have a car pick you up at seven a.m. be ready."

## Claimed By Desire

In dramatic fashion, Bryson walked out the door to the driver that was waiting for him in a black Lincoln Town Car.

# *SEVEN*

EVERY STEP BRYSON TOOK felt like he was walking on hot jagged nails. He tried being nice, he tried being mean, but still he got nowhere with Allison. He slid into the waiting car and slammed the door. He could have simply gotten the boxes of files he needed himself, and delivered them to her, but maybe if he had her in a place where she couldn't keep running away from him, they could hash it out.

"Take me home Ronald...Dammit!" Bryson used his fists to slam the back seat of the lincoln town car he was being ushered home in. The driver, Ronald in his black chauffeur hat glanced back at him through the rear view mirror. Then he pressed a button that made a clear glass rise up between them. Bryson sometimes got this way and he usually knew why. More times than not it was because he lost a large sum of money on a 'new can't fail' venture. Bryson had many wins in business, but more losses than he would care to remember.

*What am I going to do now?* he thought. Maybe he hadn't tried hard enough and maybe he'd hurt her, but she had no right keeping something so important from him. As his thoughts drifted towards a happier outcome than he was on track for, his cell phone vibrated. He looked down at his caller id and the picture of Laura came on the screen.

His head started to hurt as soon as he saw her. What was he going to do with Laura? His trusted advisor and confidant for over twenty years would be furious at his predicament. She would probably suggest getting his child by court order, but he wanted to avoid such a nasty outcome.

The arrangement they had, that they've been working on for months now, seemed....wrong. Lately, Laura was hinting she should be more than his advisor.

The report from the exploratory committee was simple. If he wanted to run for office, it would be best to get married. Laura threw her name in the hat before Bryson could think if he wanted to go that route.

Someone, without his consent had leaked info to the press about him and Laura, now mock ups of their potential children were appearing on blogs of those who cared about such things. The entire thing was making him awfully uncomfortable when they were together, but she was an exceptional advisor, and great friend.

"Yeah."

"Hi Bryson where are you? We were suppose to go to Le Chateau tonight for dinner?"

That's right, Bryson was so caught up with Allison that he totally forgot about the dinner.

"Oh that's right. Sorry something came up that I had to take care of."

"Well you should have called, I was all dressed up with no where to go."

She was flirting.

Bryson chuckled and said, "you have succeeded in making me feel badly. Can we postpone or is there something you wanted to go over tonight?" Awkward relationship or not, things still had to get done.

Lauren replied "um...let me see. I don't know...Our reservation was for seven, why don't you come over here and we'll go over what Sanders recommended. "

Bryson knew what Sanders, one of his lawyers recommenced and he didn't like it one bit. He still hadn't decided if public office was worth the price on his personal life. However, he needed to get his mind off Allison and work was a sure way to do it, he hoped.

"Alright, I can be there in fifteen minutes."

Covering the phone, Bryson knocked on the pane glass separating himself from the driver and mouthed "Laura's house," then went back to the conversation.

"Have you eaten? Should I stop and pick something up for you?" One thing about knowing someone for more than half their life is knowing what they liked to eat. "I can bring chinese over if you're hungry."

"No, I'm alright... You're all I need right now...to go over these suggestions."

Lauren was really cool, he loved her in every way except as a lover or Wife.

If only.

"See you in a bit."

He hung up the phone with a heavy heart. In all his years, things had never been so complicated.

As Bryson was on his way to Lauren's house, Allison was back at her hotel suite pouring her heart out to her best friend.

"I'm tired of being an emotional reck! Jeez!" Allison paced back and forth from the small kitchen to the television in the joint living room of their suite provided by her company. The cheery yellow walls and floral couches reminded her of Florida when she went there for spring break a few years ago.

"I mean in the last two days, I've wanted to cry, yell, sleep, eat, and behead someone, at least twice. What is wrong with me. I have more control than this!"

The last statement exaggerated with an up and down arm movement that made Sam her best friend put down the Shape magazine she was holding, and really start to pay attention.

Alli-"

"I mean I calm down and every time I see HIM, he manages to turn out worse that he was the last time, and let me tell you, that's not an easy thing to do."

"Allison, sweetie listen, stop for a minute just stop."

"Stop What?" Now Allison's wrath was directed at her friend. "Stop What? I can't stop. I'm still pregnant with a man's baby who I hate and may I remind you who I have to work with for the next 4 days, I can't stop."

Allison did something she rarely did. She flopped on one of the floral couches and started bawling her eyes out.

Sam rushed over, sat next to her best friend and placed her head in her lap. She stayed quiet as Allison cried thick heavy tears.

"It will be OK Alli, trust me, everything will be OK. You are going through it now, and I know you can't see clear to the next five minutes, but take my word for it, this too shall pass." Allison just moaned when she heard that.

"Look, remember when we were stranded in New Orleans with no money and no way to get home."

Allison remembered. It wasn't a topic she wanted to think about. In hindsight it was not a smart thing to do. At the time, they were freshmen at the University of Georgia itching for some "adventure". They found it in two guys they met at the Varsity, a local restaurant, who were on their way to the Essence music festival in New Orleans.

The guys, Rob and Marlo, invited them along promising fun, sun and music. What they hadn't promised was a way back home and companionship while there. They reached New Orleans and the guys disappeared after they used up all the girls money for gas and the hotel stay during the trip.

The two trusting college freshmen were stranded in New Orleans with little money, no place to stay, and a city-wide party going on around them.

She stayed quiet and Sam continued. "You thought it was the end of the world. You didn't think you could take another breath or live another day but we got through it."

"That's different. First of all it was both of us so we were able to think about it and figure out how to get home. Plus, we could have just called one of our parents and it would have been fine--"

"But neither one of us wanted to do that. Which one of us wanted to go through that. If they found out what we did, we'd still be under punishment."

If it wasn't for a classmate Sabrina, and western union, they'd probably still be in the Bayou.

"That's not the point Alli, it's that we banded together and made it happen. Neither one of us folded and died, it passed, like this will. Remember how we thought it was the end...well it wasn't."

"That was us. This is me, all me. You aren't the one that's pregnant Sam, you're not the one whose going through this, it's me. You can't help me get out of this! You aren't the one who is going to be disowned by her parents and who will probably lose her job after this, it's me. How could you possibly understand." Allison sat up "This is my fault. I am here because of me." She covered her eyes with her hands and burst into a new set of tears.

Those words hurt a little. Sam and Alli were inseparable. Alli's pain was her pain as she hoped her's was experienced by her friend.

"Is that why you're so angry? Because you are staring in your own pity party. The perfect, 'never made a mistake in her life' girl has made a mistake? Are you upset because this long held image of yourself that you are above doing anything wrong is coming to bite you in the ass?"

What Alli said really rubbed Sam the wrong way.

"Whoa there Sam. Why are you getting so snippy? All this perfect talk is bull and you know it."

Allison didn't dwell on Sam's outburst. They'd had this argument back and forth for years. Each one thinking the other had a perfection complex.

"Anyway, don't look at me like that! Angry, come on! What do you mean is that why I'm angry? Can't you tell?"

"I want to hear it from you," said Sam.

"I'm angry because I hate Bryson, but yet I still have to be around him."

"You don't have to do anything you don't want to." Sam stared at Allison without flinching.

What is that suppose to mean?"

"It means you can go online and book a ticket out of here and go back to Atlanta tomorrow. You don't ever have to see Bryson again."

"Boy does that sound good," said Allison as she dried her cheeks with a napkin, "but I have to stay." Allison walked into the kitchen for some water, came back and turned on the television.

"No you don't."

"If I don't stay and finish this, I'm liable to get fired. I'm not on track to employee of the month. Far from it. Plus, I think Andrew is out for my head. I refuse to let that crumb snatcher anywhere near it."

"My point sticks, you don't have to stay, you want to. You are going through this because of your job. Don't act like you don't have a choice." Samantha was facing her now. Standing short at five feet three inches in front of Allison, not giving an inch.

"Semantics Sam, I also have to pay my half of the mortgage for our apartment," said Allison as she paced around the room, putting things away as she talked so she wouldn't have to look straight at her challenging friend.

"We'll make it. There is always a way. Plus, you can always come and work for me for a bit until you find another job if you lose this one, which you won't. But, ff you can't take it, if you can't handle Bryson then quit and leave." Sam stared at Allison with a puppy dog look on her face, knowing full well what she just did.

"Samantha Vanessa Morgan, do not mock me. This is serious. Why are you taunting me?"

"Who me?" With a beginning smirk on her face, Samantha picked up the shape magazine she was reading and started leafing through it innocently.

"Yes you. I don't quit and I don't give up. I see what you did. I guess I needed to snap out of it." With an all encompassing sigh, Allison flopped down on the chair.

"What am I going to do? How am I going to get through the rest of this week?"

"The same way you've gotten through every other less than ideal moment in your life. You are going to suck it up and take it minute by minute and get through it. Before you know it, it will be done, and you can move on."

"I'll try, it's just that Bryson knows how to grate on my inner nerves. I think he has an MBA in pushing me to the brink of madness." Allison went to the balcony to stare out at the faded lights of the cruise ships on the ocean. The wind felt good going through her hair.

"Let me ask you, are you going to tell him?"

Words Allison didn't want to touch. When he wasn't around, when she could demonize him as a degenerate less than human person, she wasn't faced with that question. Now he was around and determined to be friends or something. He wanted to talk which was the last thing Allison wanted.

"Tell him what? I've said everything to him I've wanted to tell him already." Almost everything. She really wanted to know why he'd left her. What she said in the restaurant was just subterfuge.

"You know what I mean, tell him about his baby."

"It's not his baby, it's My baby."

"Allison, don't be stupid. He has a right to know."

"Right my ass! He had a right to not leave after he used me that night, so I don't want to hear it. This little baby is going up for adoption."

*What about my rights?* Thought Allison.

"What if you have the baby and don't want to give it up, what are you going to do then?"

Sam had a way of fleshing out all the things Allison didn't want to talk about. Little by little, day by day, morning sickness by morning sickness, Allison was starting to look forward to the little growing person. She was developing a connection, a slight yearning to this new being and she didn't know how to deal with it.

She told herself it didn't matter, that she wouldn't be a good mother, that she didn't want to raise a baby by herself. Not a girl from a good family, with a great education and career.

Not her! Part of it was her embarrassment of what people would think, what others would say, how they would judge. She partly believed it the potential backlash she would get.

"I don't want to talk about this anymore."

"You have to deal with this, you can't keep pushing things away. It's his baby too Allison, regardless of how much you don't want it to be."

"Have you eaten? I'm full. The one good thing about tonight is I had some really good food." Allison busied herself with looking at the hotel folder of available restaurants.

"You can put me off now, but you have a life growing inside of you that will not be ignored, and who has a father who needs to know what is going on."

*Yeah. I know.*

## *EIGHT*

"YEAH?"

"It's Me."

"I know who it is, what do you want?"

"I need some information."

"About?"

"You know, Bryson."

"I've been thinking about this whole thing and I don't want any part of it."

"It's too late."

"Do what you will but I'm out."

"Would that wife of yours agree with you, or how about one of those sons."

"Don't you dare threaten my family. I told you, I don't want anything to do with this anymore. I've already told you too much already.

"I'm not dicking around here. this isn't personal and I will do what I must."

"I didn't know you would turn out like this. How has it gotten to this?"

"When you are old and gray you can sit and ponder. Now I need you to shut up and listen."

"I'm listening."

"I need you to tell me which hanger Bryson has."

"His plane?"

"Which hanger is his at the airport, that's all."

"I don't know."

"Well maybe your wife knows, I'll just ask her, talk to you--"

"It's space 3394"

"Wow, you learn fast."

Then, the call ended.

Samantha was leaving in the morning to go back to Atlanta. The chance to get away from her business was fantastic, but Samantha knew if she was gone another day, she'd probably not have a real estate brokerage to go back to. Allison laid in bed with only her panties on. The air conditioning was too cold but no conditioning was too hot. the ceiling fan felt good on her nipples and skin which seemed to be more sensitive now that she was pregnant.

Her lodgings were very posh. It must have been at least a four star resort. Alli was lucky, her room faced the ocean. She got up and opened the door to let the fresh ocean breeze flow through her room. She loved the salty fresh breeze of the ocean. It relaxed her. Prepping for an early morning, she went back to bed and tried to sleep but she couldn't. Her mind kept going back to the night that was the root of her current dilemma.

He'd taken her hand as they walked up the steep hill to Peachtree Street.

"Why in the name of all that is good do so many streets have Peach or Peachtree in it's name?" Allison looked around playfully looking for who he was talking to. Realizing he was talking to her she said,

"Don't ask me, I'm not from here. Though I don't think if you were from here you'd know either."

"Where are you from?"

"New York."

"The city?"

"No."

"Where?"

"Just outside the city. It's a small little city."

"It sounds like you're embarrassed about where you're from."

"No, It's just that when people hear I'm from New York, They immediately think New York City. The lights, Broadway, the Museums, all of that. But when I tell them I lived in a little city upstate, they usually get bored."

"I could never get bored with you." Allison looked at Daniels golden eyes as they bore into her. A smile sneaked onto her face and she looked down at her feet before she was able to control it.

The butterflies started in her stomach. This gorgeous man, with his golden eyes and dark curly hair was staring at her with such intensity she started to get hot. That was a feat because it was pretty cold for the south at thirty four degrees. She trembled as the wind blew her thick curly hair away from her face.

He opened his ankle length cashmere and wool coat and pulled Allison close. He included her under his coat and hugged her to keep the cold out.

"Did I warm you up?" His  deep smoky voice was dangerously close to her ear as he said it. The brush of his breath against her ear had the blood rushing to Allison's nipples. Maybe he would think it was the cold affecting them as they were. The stubble of his five o clock shadow just starting to appear on his face confirmed Daniel was no boy.

He was a man.

 A tall, gorgeous man with a hard body as evidenced by their bodies fitting into each other as they walked. She felt engulfed not only in the warmth of his coat, but in his scent which was all over the coat, and now all over her. He didn't wear cologne, but she did smell his aftershave. He smelled like a clean cool breeze in the meadow after a summer shower mixed with cinnamon.

"Yes.... you've actually made me  quite hot." What was she saying? She never did this. This was crazy. This was wrong. It was so wrong.

"You're teasing me huh?,"said Daniel as he used his index finger to tickle her, "If you continue talking like that, I'm going to be forced to put you over my knee and spank you like the bad girl you are." He focused on her lips with a wicked grin on his face then squeezed her ass as they entered the hotel.

They reached the W hotel and he held the door for her as they went in. It was Saturday so everyone who was anyone was at the W. No music played but the buzz of the conversations and the click of glasses and bottles made it's own rhythm. She was happy to have some distance between her and Daniel. Everything was definitely moving too fast.

They walked in and took a seat at the far corner of the bar, and watched the people come and go. She was afraid of what was happening, and what seemed to be happening so fast. But the thrill, the excitement of the moment kept her going, kept her wondering where this would go.

She liked that she was good at her job, but it's no secret accounting never made Allison's panties wet. She was a good girl. The girl that did her homework, the girl that paid all her bills on time, the girl that did what her parents told her to do, the girl that didn't take risks, (except that one time, and look where that got her). It had gotten her to an okay place. She had a good job, good friends, and great parents. However, no fire burned in her for anyone or anything. Nothing cooled the sexual fire when it came roaring through her body, as it was right now.

He ordered a Jack Daniels on the rocks and she ordered an Apple Martini. The tart drink felt good going down. The kick of the alcohol loosened her inhibitions and her tongue. After hours of talking she said,

"What did you mean by spanking me?"

"Is that what you've been thinking over there? I thought you were more innocent than that. I'm the one trying to corrupt you, but I think it's too late."

The challenge in his smile made Alli's back stiffen. If he wanted to play, they could play.

"You don't know how innocent or naughty I am.....yet."

She loved this. Alli could swear she saw him growl at her, but it went by so fast, she thought she imagined it.

"Do you want something to eat?" He asked.

"I have a taste for something ...ah...savory and sweet. Something that's going to fill me up again and again. A taste for something that's going to make me filled and satisfied after I've had it."

With a sly smile, Alli looked pointedly at Daniel. He stayed quiet for a while watching Alli, tracking her every move, ready to pounce. He took a drink of his Jack, never taking his eyes off her.

"What are we doing here?... I like you," said Daniel.

"You don't know me."

"What is there to know?"

"My age."

"How old are you?"

"Twenty Four. How old are you?"

"I'm Thirty Seven." She knew he was older than her but she hadn't thought about a specific age. There was a moment of concern than he was too old, but it came and went like the wind. The concern was replaced by the sexual thrill of being handled by an older man.

"Are you married?" asked Alli.

"No. Are you married?"

"No." *No where near it*, thought Alli. He got up and sat next to her in the booth.

"Can I touch you?" The heat behind Alli's eyes blurred her vision and her head went back slightly at the simple but erotic request.

Coming from Daniel, with his smell coalescing around her, filling her with his scent, she longed to be filled with something more. She wouldn't back down now. She'd come too far.

"Yes..."she whispered.

It was loud enough for his ears only. The buzz of the crowd at the bar ceased to exist. The people disappeared. The only sound were the moans coming from Allison as Daniel's hands snaked below her sweater to rest on her breast. The thirty four Ds filled Daniel's palm and he approved by squeezing. Before Alli could make any noise to attract attention, Daniel covered her mouth with his and kissed the last of Alli's remaining doubt away.

The spark of desire rose slowly. Engulfing her body little by little, touch by touch, bite by bite. Then it built into an inferno. Daniels lips were so soft they felt like marshmallows and tasted just as sweet. She yielded to his tongue as it searched for entrance between her lips. Allison didn't think about anything, didn't see anything, other than fireworks behind her closed eyes.

As they kissed, Daniel teased Alli's nipples and pulled on her hair softly with his other hand. The moans came more and more as Alli tried to take it all in. She tried to regulate the barrage of emotions, but her body had other plans. Her body was going for it.

She reached between his legs for the steadily increasing bulge that grew with ever squeeze of her nipple as she moaned into their kiss. She firmly stroked him, alternatively squeezing and rubbing his hardness until he couldn't take it anymore.

"You're teasing me again." He signaled for the check and fixed his pants.

"And what do you propose to do about it Daniel?"

"Come on, I'll show you," he said while getting one last feel before he got up. He paid the bill and reached for her hand.

She could end it all here. She could leave him, they could go their separate ways, no hard feelings. She glanced up at him. His face was illuminated by the bar. He looked like a naughty pleasure encased in fun. Gorgeous manly fun.

She placed her hand in his, and knew her life would never be the same again.

The elevator ride was agonizing. Bryson had his floor length coat in his hand as he leaned against the back wall of the elevator. Allison stood in front of him, teasing him softly with her hips. A soft chuckle escaped his lips a few times on the way to the Penthouse suite. He bent down to her ears and whispered, "You will pay for this."

The words went to her core. Yes, she wanted to pay for it, over and over again. She pushed against him harder, with more urgency. She reached for his hand and guided it to rest under her sweater on her stomach.

She would've gone further if it wasn't for the elderly couple standing beside them.

She wanted him so badly she could taste it, touch it. Anticipation was building. How would he feel? How would he taste? How far would she go? These questions loomed in her mind as the elevators rose to the Penthouse level of the hotel.

She saw him in the elevator panels' reflection. He stood behind her confident, and deliciously sexy. Bryson's dark blue suit hung perfectly on his sculpted body, screaming power both in the boardroom and the bedroom.

The elevator opened directly into a foyer in front of the door to his penthouse suite. No hallway or other suite was available. A place that needed a key from the elevator just to reach it. Without hesitation, Bryson pulled Alli from the elevators before if closed and he drove her to the delicately wallpapered walls, threw his coat on the floor and proceeded to explore his prize. His hand cupped her cheek, exploring, rubbing her soft delicate skin. She moaned in response.

"You're Beautiful."

Allison let out the breath she didn't know she was holding. His eyes told her he was telling the truth. She felt special, prized, valued.

"I..uh.."

He didn't let her finished. He covered her lips with his. Swiping his tongue between her lips, tasting her sweetness. Their tongues danced together in harmony. Their bodies fitting together better than either of them had imagined. Her soft frame against his hard body.

"I'm going to make you pay for all your teasing," he said while he nipped at her neck.

Allison froze.

In between his strong embrace, she felt consumed, covered by him, she knew she was in trouble and welcomed it.

"Yeah? Sure." She was teasing him again. He gave her a wry look. Without warning, he picked her up. She straddled him with her back against the wall. Surprise and arousal traveled through her, threatening loud moans of desire. But, she dampened her emotions and replied.

"So, you're a little strong."

He grinned. His erection grinded into her, hard and urgent. His hands went under her sweater and pulled it over her head. Her red bra was a flimsy obstacle for what he wanted. He used his mouth to caress her neck and lips. His teeth nipped her hard nipple through the lace bra causing Allison to stiffen in his arms.

When he used his mouth to expose her breasts to him, he licked them one by one, slowly, seductively, making the air around them cause Allison tortuous pleasure.

He put Allison down for a second, so he could take her pants off, which he did with surprising speed. Only her panties were left. He hoisted her back up against the wall enjoying her big firm tits.

"Tonight I'm fu-loving you." The declaration sent fire up Alli's spine. Allison was a mound of moans and soft erotic curses edging him on. He licked his finger and slipped it under her damp panties to rest at her entrance. Everything stopped for Allison. Their eyes locked, deep and golden with dark and piercing.

"Um..." said Allison. Her words lost, covered by his lips while he slipped his wet finger inside her. Her body clenched at the welcomed invasion.

She wanted more. She moved her hips around, begging for more with her body. He responded by slipping another finger inside her. She moaned and used her teeth to bite his neck. He answered by rubbing her clit.

Allison lost it. The lust Bryson woke in her, made her sexual energy explode into aggression. She pulled his suit jacket off, then went to remove his shirt. She wanted to feel his chest.

When he was naked, she used her tongue to lick his chest and nipples. She felt free, her instincts guiding her. She bit his nipple and he slammed her harder against the wall.

"Don't do that."

"Why not? Can't take it?"

"You don't learn do you?"

He placed Allison back on the floor and turned her around so she faced the wall.

"You are making me do this."

Bryson bent her over, spread her legs and used his fingers to play at her opening.

"Oh" screamed Allison, but Bryson wasn't letting up.

He licked his fingers again and placed them in Allison. She was moaning incomprehensibly.

"I told you not to tease me." Bryson held Allison bent over, legs open with one hand and used the other to spank her ass hard enough to sting, but not hard enough to hurt.

The sensation made Allison's knees buckle.

"Stand up, I'm not done with you yet."

He palmed her ass then slapped it again a little harder the second time around. She let out a moan so loud, she was glad they were the only ones on the floor.

"Say it?" another palm and slap on her round ass. Almost all brain function ceased to exist, but she heard his prompt.

"Say what?"

"That you want me." It wasn't a question. Her core was wet with desire. Creamy with need.

"I want you." she whispered.

"I didn't hear you."

"I want you."

"To do what?"

"Whatever you want."

"Oo, that's a good girl." He used his fingers to caress her.

"But what do you want me to do specifically."

Her mind was a blank. Her brain was trying to understand the fireworks erupting throughout her body. Small nuclear blasts where going off between her entrance, to her nipples. Soft curses made Bryson harden more than he already was.

"Fu-love me."

"How?" Allison knew what she wanted and he was going to make her say it.

"With your---" He cut her off as he thrust his erection inside her.

Her knees buckled and he had to hold her up. Her world was buzzing with sensation. He flled her up entirely. His hard thrusts were engulfed by her softness, massaging him, comforting him, baiting him to give up his very essence.

They got into a rhythm, her hips meeting his at the intersection of utter and complete pleasure. He reached into her hair and pulled slightly. He felt her tighten up, felt her body stiffen at her pending release.

She was close.

He pulled out all the way. Allison looked back at him. He used his hardness to tease her opening. Curses left her mouth.

He grinned a naughty grin.

Daniel loved to be in control, but he knew if he played much longer, he would lose his audience. He pushed into her, breaking the coils of tension he'd built up within her. Allison's body crumbled into a mass of ecstatic convulsions ravaging through her body.

He followed right behind her. His body releasing everything he had with a loud groan. After the stars stopped dancing in front of their eyes, they both slid to the floor. Allison put her head on his shoulder and he hugged her, stroking her hair in the process. There was nothing to be said except.

"WOW," said Allison.

A cocky look came across Daniel's face.

Allison laughed and got up to gather her clothes.

"Are we going in or," waving her hands taking in the small area they were in, " is this it?" A satiated and satisfied smile lit up her face.

Daniel sat up, lifted Allison into his arms and carried her into the penthouse suite. He walked into the master bedroom and dropped her on the bed with a bounce. Once Allison stopped bouncing and laughing she went to the shower. The day started out exciting, promising a great new home, and was ending as one of the best times of Allison's young life.

She came in from the shower relaxed. Plush carpeting surrounding her toes, made her at home. The living room had three soft plush couches with a table in between. The flat screen television was mounted on the wall beside the floor to ceiling windows, framing the skyline of Atlanta at dark.

While Allison showered, Daniel had room service bring up three bottles of Dom Perignon champagne, strawberries, grapes, cheese and crackers. The lights were dim which made the view of the city take over the room.

It was breathtakingly beautiful.

"For me?" ssked Allison, when she saw the spread.

"Oh This? No way. I always do this. You just happen to be here," said Daniel with a sly smile.

He took her hand and walked to the window. A current flowed from his fingers up her arms. Allison looked out of the window, staring at the thousands of lights and buildings that greeted her, falling back onto Daniels hard body.

She was peaceful. All was right with the world.

He reached around and untied Alli's robe and dropped it to the ground.

So, Bryson wasn't finished for the night.

"What are you thinking?" he asked.

Without turning her around he explored her body with achingly slow movements. His hands were strong but soft as they reached her thigh then travelled up to her breasts.

"You touching me."

Allison closed her eyes no longer seeing the city, its energy pulsating through her body. The stubble from Daniels beard reached Allison's neck. His tongue wrapped around her ear while he squeezed and teased her body.

"Oh." Shocks vibrated through her body and soft sweet juice flowed to her thigh as she let Daniel claim her. To surrender herself to him felt natural, felt right.

Her hips instinctively moved rhythmically against his, corresponding to the desire traveling through her body. He moved to her neck, savoring the taste of her. His left hand found her hair and he pulled lightly as he nicked her neck seductively. She groaned her approval and soft curses left her lips.

"You taste good," said Allison.

With a possessive movement, Daniel captured Allison's left leg and placed it on the chair next to them. She loosened her body, surrendering to being molded by Daniel and whatever he wanted to do with her. He kissed down her body, until he reached her ass. He tilted it so he could get a good view of her sweet core.

"You're pretty everywhere aren't you?" He leaned her forward and ravaged her entrance with his tongue, licking, fondling her with ever flick.

Alli reached for the glass pane windows to hold herself up. Strong hands held her in place because her bones had turned to liquid.

He went deeper and explored more with his tongue. Sucking on the soft flesh of Alli's erotic zone, Daniel made

Alli scream with pleasure that felt so good she couldn't take it. Her skin buzzed from her toes to the top of her head. She tried to move and get away but his strong arms kept her in place. She had to get away from the overload of sensations.

He bent her over and inhaled Alli's slick scent. Looking at him while he did that drove Allison mad. It looked so erotic. Their eyes met. That only made him harder. She smelled savory, and tasted like honey.

When their eyes met, her insides melted. Working his magic against Alli's legs, Daniel was rewarded when Allison's knees got week and she slipped to the floor.

Bryson's urgency increased.

He flipped her over and kissed her lips, tasting her sweetness. Then he stopped and just stared at her welcoming body for a few seconds before he moved.

He opened her legs with his body, raining kisses along her neck. Allison wrapped her hands around his back urging him, wanting him to take her. She throbbed with need, as she waited for him to enter her, not knowing when it would be. The anticipation had her body buzzing.

Softly and gently, Daniel used his erection to circle Alli's opening. He was rewarded with her erotic moans. He covered her mouth with his in a sensuous kiss, as he softly and gently filled her up.

Light flashed behind his closed eyes and he jerked away from her mouth. Their connection turned Daniel's body into an electricity conductor.

"No one's ever made me...feel the way you do," said Daniel. Allison melted at his words.

Opening her mouth with his finger he entered her again, harder. She sucked on his fingers. Her tongue wrapping around them as she pumped into her.

He watched as her tongue made love to his fingers, while he pumped into her soft wet core. Her body accepted in, surrendered to his invasion.

She gripped his back and trembled. Staring into her deep brown eyes, he released her mouth and whispered in her ear.

"You're...amazing."

A primal urge grew in Daniel with every stroke he took.

She was his.

He wanted to claim her, possess her, all of her. His chest expanded between gasps of realization. He wanted her in every way, body, mind, and soul. Between moans of pleasure he said.,"that's it, you're now mine."

It wasn't a question, but a fact he felt to share with Allison.

Alli didn't answer.

Daniels rhythm increased as well as his connection to Allison.

"No one else is allowed in you again." The strength of his thrusts got harder, firmer.

"Did you hear me." He slapped Allison's ass for effect.

"I said no man but me will enter you. You are mine."

"Yes, Daniel. Yes."

He watched her bite her lips and tense up. She was trying to hold on, not if he had anything to do with it.

"Mine."

His rhythm increased and he took her legs and put them on his shoulders without pulling out. Her eyes widened as she felt him go further inside of her. Panic crossed her face and he pulled out a little.

"Wait..." Tentatively, Alli pushed Daniel away. She looked afraid of the dept he was reaching. He was trying to touch her emotionally, he needed her to trust him not to hurt her.

"Look at me." She slowly looked at him. He bore into Allison's soul with his piercing eyes.

"Do you trust me?"

"Yes." His heart soared.

"I want you to relax." He saw her hesitation. He felt how tight she held her body and realized she was not relaxing. He reached for one of her feet and brought it to his mouth. Slowly, he took his tongue and licked her toes one by one, as he slowly and gently rocked back and forth inside her. A low guttural sound escaped her body and liquid heat flowed around his erection.

Looking back at her, he concentrated on her eyes.

"Let go....and trust me."

Alli's head went back. She looked so torn. He looked at her, light bouncing off her skin coming from the floor to ceiling window. Her soft heart shaped face tugged at him, he wanted to protect her, and help her to be unafraid.

"I won't hurt you Allison. Let me in." The sound of his deep voice bouncing off the walls like a soft trumpet playing the sweetest jazz made her breath catch. He rocked a littler harder and a littler further into Allison, but she didn't protest. His hands explored her body slowly, enjoying her silk soft skin. He inhaled her sweet smell. He reached her breasts, cupped them, and gently plucked her nipple as he thrust into her, a little harder, and a little deeper. Daniel filled her up inside and out. His hardness filling every soft corner of her core.

"I want you Allison."

Allison moaned and stared up at Daniel. The moment so intense, words would be awkward.

The air felt thick, and hot.

He saw neither the room they were in, nor the skyline. Every inch of Alli's body shook, trying to make sense of the myriad of emotions rolling off her.

"Can I have you?"

He couldn't fully claim her if she didn't want to be claimed. What a question. He watched her tense up again.

"Only..."

Allison paused and let out a little scream as her buildup of ecstasy in her body started to bubble over. Every great emotion she'd ever felt started to gather just under her chest and existed all the way to her entrance. Her skin was on fire. Happiness, joy, ecstasy, fulfillment, pride, all rolled up into one, increased in her gut with every thrust of Daniel into her.

"Only what Kitten," said Daniel, hesitant and unsure of where Allison was going.

"Only... if you promise.... to catch me when I fall."

That simple and innocent plea pulled and shattered Daniels heart. He looked at Alli's face, honest and good, sweet, with a hint of honey. He didn't know what hit him or where it came from. He thought the things he felt took years to develop, but he decided as he looked down at Allison with ecstasy rolling off of her, that she was his. He would spend the rest of his life catching her, protecting her, loving her, and making her happy.

As he filled her up and felt every inch of Allison in her most compromising position, he recognized that she was the one for him, the one who completed him. The only one who ever touched him to his core.

"I got you kitten. I will always have you. Let me in." Daniel barely got that out as he released years of the wrong women, years of gold diggers, years of being along. His orgasm shattered the last of his reserve, and he let out a growl that made the hairs at the back of Allison's neck raise. At the same time, the ecstasy that was built up in Allison spilled over, and Allison went with it.

Daniel covered her mouth with his and kissed her gently and sensually, as her body tensed for what seemed like hours. He rode her orgasm until she couldn't see straight.

She actually forgot how to breath. Her brain was silent as her body took over. Waves of bliss washed over her body as she came from a climax that had her seeing stars. As they both came down from the best love making either of them had ever had, Daniel fell beside her and hugged Allison close. It seemed like hours before either of them spoke.

They just enjoyed each other's bodies. He stroked her hair and she nuzzled into his body, as they lay looking at the skyline.

"I meant what I said you know." The deep rumble of a sated man, had the blood rushing through Allison again.

"Yeah?"

"Yeah." The smile across Allison's face could light a small country. She was so happy at that moment, she didn't know what to do with herself. She nuzzled into him closer, and started to stroked his arm.

"What do we do now?"

"I don't know about you, but I'm going to take it second by second, because I don't want to rush or miss anything with you," said Daniel.

"Yeah?"

"Yeah." Happy she wasn't the only one that felt this way, she fitted her self perfectly onto Daniels body and looked out the floor to ceiling windows.


Back in her hotel room in the Cayman Islands and her current predicament, Allison punched the wet pillow she was laying on, and turned it over to the dry side.

She didn't realized she was crying.

She felt broken. Everything was wrong and there was going to be no easy answer. A man, whom she now felt she foolishly gave in to the first time she met him, a man she didn't know, a man who she let it all go for, had betrayed her.

He left her in that cold bed the next morning, alone. He'd rejected all she'd given him. He didn't want the piece of herself that she put out there.

"He promised," she screamed to no one. But who was she kidding. Ads on TV promised weight loss with magic pills. Everyone promised something and everyone Allison was starting to see, lied. But he didn't just use her body, play with her emotion and leave her, he left her with a part of himself growing inside of her.

# *NINE*

BRYSON'S LIMO CAME TO a halt in front of Lauren's Condo.

Lauren.

A heavy sigh escaped Bryson. His head fell back on the soft leather seats trying to figure out what he was going to do with Lauren. He put the divider up, rolled down the window, and lit a cigarette. He knew this introspective period could take a while.

He looked up at the night sky through the sun roof, searching for guidance, Bryson found nothing but darkness with small specks of far away lights.

Allison Caine, a firecracker, his auditor, his pain in the ass, the mother of his child.

Now what?

Bryson felt the food he just ate start to attack him. Allison was giving him ageda, heart burn.

He needed Tums ten minutes ago. Maybe the acid would burn his vocal cords so badly he wouldn't have to say anything to anyone ever again. They would sympathize with him and not hold him to his actions. Although, Bryson found that few people sympathized with a billionaire.

A sharp pounding started at his temple. He used his hand to knead it back down, but it wouldn't comply. The stars offered nothing, so he closed his eyes.

Lauren, tall, beautiful, sweet, and the heir to the Williamson Empire greeted him behind his eye lids.

Beside her, his mother.

At seven years old Bryson was beat up in school by a group of kids older than he was. When Antoinette, his mother heard about it, she calmly sat Bryson down with a bag of ice on his eye, and asked him how much he had in his piggy bank.

He didn't know so his Mother told him to go get it. Bryson returned with a porcelain blue dinosaur piggy bank. While he was gone Antoinette had gotten the hammer. She sat Bryson down and asked,

"How did it feel to get beat up?"

"Terrible" replied little Bryson.

"Who watched?" ask Antoinette

"Half the school was there," said Bryson before bursting into tears. The sting of the cut under his eyes made the crying harder to handle.

If Bryson thought the sting from his tears hurt, his mother was all but shattering inside. Her baby, beaten by stupid imbeciles.

After the crying stopped enough so Antoinette could get a word in she asked,

"What do you want to do about this?"

"What can I do, they are bigger than me and there are so many of them."

With a firm hand, Antoinette held Bryson still and looked into her baby's golden eyes and said,

"You can always do something. Always. It doesn't matter how big they are or how many of them their are, you are an Anderson, and no one beats us. Do you understand?"

Bryson wanted to act brave and answer with a rallying war cry but he didn't mean it. His mother wasn't there, she didn't feel Brad's fist connect to his eye, or Shep's kick to the groin. She didn't even have a groin like he did, how could she possibly understand. So he just stared at her.

Realizing she was getting no where, Antoinette tried another tactic. "

"Do you want to knock those kids in the head?"

"Of course I do," frustrated with the conversation, Bryson started to pace around the living room. All he wanted to do right now was to go back to his room and lick his wounds.

"So why don't you?"

"I already told you, I'm too small."

Bryson couldn't understand why she couldn't understand, why would she want to torture him all over again. He guessed it was the national parent pastime. How to torture your kids, especially after a traumatizing situation 101.

"Who said you have to do it. You may be just one person, but that's not the only way to get things done.

Usually if you can't stand it or you're unable to skin the cat yourself, you have someone else do."

"No one is going to do it for me. Everyone is scared of them."

Antoinette reached for the hammer, looked from Bryson to the porcelain piggy bank and then straight at him. It took a minute for little Bryson to understand but when he did a look of horror came across his face.

"Mom! I can't do that! You want me to pay someone to beat up Brad and his buddies? That's crazy! First of all I wouldn't know who to get and how to do it. or if that's even right. Is this a test or something? Why would you say that?"

"Do you want to walk around the school scared until you leave? You will be afraid at every point in your life. It's either you take care of this now, or it will haunt you for years to come. Look sweetheart, life is not sunshine and roses all the time, if you want to make an omelet, you've gotta break a couple of eggs."

Antoinette placed the hammer on the table next to the dinosaur full of coins and bills and walked out.

No one at Wilson Academy ever bothered Bryson again.

Bryson sat up after wasting time sitting in the back of his car, acting like that hurt seven year old boy, and reached for the door. He remembered his mother's words, but how could he break a couple of eggs if she was one of them.

She was the one trying to couple him and Lauren. She thought it a perfect combination of power and beauty.

Antoinette Anderson was the force behind his family's fortune. Everyone knew, if it wasn't for her, Anderson Sr. would not be where he was, and neither would Bryson. Fierce and determined, Antoinette feared no one, but made knees around the world buckle, especially if someone happened to be in her crosshairs.

She loved Bryson more than she loved herself, and wanted the world for him. She figured as her time in this life grew shorter, Lauren would be ideal in continuing all of her hard work, elevating her family to even higher heights.

How could her only son tell her that he was going against her, that all her carefully laid plans were for naught?

But Lauren wasn't the one that made his heart skip, she was the one giving him heart burn. He refused to settle for power when he could have a family. Now he had to figure out how to get it.

At Lauren's door, Bryson wondered if he would be able to do what he came to do. Could he end it all here and now?

He wanted Allison, he knew he had to. He couldn't have Lauren thinking there was a chance. He needed to release any baggage that would sabotage his hopefully impending family with Allison. Because Andersons' didn't fail.

He knocked.

He waited for a few seconds until an excited Lauren swung the door open.

"Hey Bry. Come on in."

He hated being called Bry, but he'd corrected her enough times. Now wasn't the right time.

"Thanks." He walked into her expensively decorated condo and closed the door behind him. He was ready.

# *TEN*

BUTTERFLIES DANCED IN BRYSON'S stomach and his mouth felt like he was just eating powder. He looked at his watch and paced back and forth in front of the stairs to his Lear Jet.

Allison had another six minutes before she was officially late. The thought that she wouldn't show up didn't occur to him until now. He had Ronald go shopping for some clothes for her and he'd clear her absence with her boss earlier. Mr. Osmund didn't mind, as long as the audit would be finished by the end of the week.

This wasn't exactly an official trip. He could have simply had someone pick up the boxes of bank statements for one of his small holding companies, but this was better.

This way, she would have to talk to him without running away. There was no running away on his Private Island.

It was a beautiful morning. Still, a little cool, but sunny.

"Bryson, my Man. How's it going?" Bryson turned around and saw Clive Williams standing in front of him.

"Clive. How are you?"

"Good, good. Where are you off to?"

"Business trip."

"What's the story with the campaign? Are you guys going to run?"

"Clive, when I decide, you will be one of the first to know." Clive was fishing.

"Alright. Ronny is looking forward to the friendly competition."

Bryson Jr. knew better. Clive would give his left nut for him not to run, and everyone knew it. Ronny was an idiot shyster, who embezzled money from the companies he was a part of. Everyone wanted him gone and Bryson thought he may be the one to do it.

"I see you look busy, I'll be going now. Don't forget to let me know."

"Yeah. Will do," said Bryson as Clive walked toward the hangers at the airport.

With thirty seconds left on the clock, Bryson saw Ronald pulling up with Allison in the back of his Lincoln Town car limousine. He couldn't help but notice how great she looked. For a moment, he let himself remember their night together back in Atlanta. Her soft skin and enthusiasm made him smile. Maybe he could get her back to that place.

"Mr. Anderson." With a nod of her head Allison brushed pass Bryson and entered the plane with the Pilot's help.

He followed her and took his seat next to her.

"There is more room over there," said Allison pointing to her right.

"I know, I want to sit beside you."

"Suit yourself." Allison put on her seat belt and looked out the window.

The Pilot went over their flight plan, weather and time of arrival. The flight would only take about an hour. Allison saw there were no attendants on the flight. Probably because the flight was so short.

"Listen, I'm sorry for the way I was the other night at the Ball."

When Allison said nothing, he continued.

"I didn't mean to come on so strong. I was only kidding. I remember how you teased me, and I was only teasing you.

A small smile crossed Allison's face before she wiped it off.

He continued, "...and that dinner last night was a little much. That's not me. Once again I'm sorry."

The Pilot announced they were ready for take off, but neither of them were paying attention.

"You know what, let's pretend this is our first meeting. We can reset, start over so to speak...Alright I'll go first. Hi, I'm Bryson, nice to meet you."

He held out his hand for Allison to take it. It hung in the air between them.

"It's too late for that. I don't pretend. It's either what is or isn't. Thanks for the apology though."

This was going to be harder than he thought. Good. What fun would it be if it was too easy. He loved that she had a backbone.

"Did you sleep well?" Asked Bryson, "...you look well rested."

"I rested good enough, you?" asked Allison with a courteous smile.

With a shrug, Bryson said "good enough." There eyes locked for a second before Allison looked away.

*It may not be too late* thought Bryon, *maybe not too late*.

Two magazines and a bottle of water later, Allison stared out at the deep blue ocean beneath her. She looked at her watch, They would be landing soon.

"How long is this going to take?" She asked.

"How long is what going to take?"

"This trip. I want to make sure we'll be back before night fall. I think traveling over the ocean at night would be a little scary. Mr. Ormond called me this morning and told this had something to do with files or something. I didn't get it all, I was already running late. So where are we going?"

"To complete the audit, I have boxes of bank statements from one of my smaller holding companies on my island, a couple hundred miles away. I figured you could look over them from there, that way they could stay there. This company is a hobby of mine and I don't want many people with access to the info. Once I take it from the island, it could get into the wrong hands."

"So you decided to bring me to the files instead of bringing the files to me."

"Basically...Plus I felt we kept being distracted, and there are some things I want to settle with you."

Allison's breath caught in her throat and her heart started to pulse in her ear.

"Like what?"

"Firstly, I want you not to hate me."

With a heavy sigh Allison said, "I don't hate you particularly.. I just..."

Just then a loud bang sounded below them. Thick dark grey to black flames started engulfing the cabin as well as outside their window. Panic made Allison frozen in fear. She couldn't even scream. Instead she gripped the seat and held on for dear life. Rushing air filled the smoke filled cabin throwing off the oxygen and balance making it hard to breath. It smelled like burning tires. Allison felt herself falling fast, nosediving into the deep blue ocean and she couldn't do anything about it. They say when death is staring you in the face, life flashes by you, but Allison's heart was in her throat and she couldn't think.

Bryson on the other hand immediately reached under his seat for the life vests. It didn't seem like there was much time, but he put the flat yellow vest over himself and pulled for inflation. Then he put one over Allison and and pulled to have it inflate. Dark grey smoke made it hard to see and it burned his throat when he tried to inhale through his mouth. He wasn't going to stop. His body moved instinctively, there was no thinking involved. He pulled the oxygen masks that flew from the ceiling on himself and Allison. Then he waited. The entire affair couldn't have lasted for more than a minute and a half but it seemed like forever.

He heard his Pilot screaming in the cockpit. Heard the rumble of the failing engines and wiz of the fast moving air around him as they nosedived. He felt the beat of his scared heart in his head, pounding letting him know he was still alive. He reached for Allison's had and held on tight. The smoke burned his nose, but it didn't hurt as much as the single tear that rolled down his cheek. He had it all, and the one thing he wanted more than money, a family was about to literally blow up into flames. He held on to Allison and closed his eyes.

Allison in her panic started crying. The fear escaping through her eyes. She didn't want to die. There were so many things she wanted to do. Things like this didn't happen to her. Her desire to live and her impending demise brought more tears from her eyes.

And what about her Baby.

The little Tyke wouldn't even get a chance to see the light of day. Two lives would perish if she died. Actually four, because her parents would likely soon follow her.

She had to live, needed to live. She wanted her baby. Alive with a chance to live, with her.

She wanted her baby.

The thought of being without the being inside of her filled her with so much loss and heart retching pain she vowed, if she made it through this, she would do what she needed to care for her baby. Their baby.

Allison looked at Bryson at that moment and squeezed his hands. As she was wrapping her fingers in his, she heard a bang intertwined with screeching bending, breaking metal and glass. A toe curling noise that reverberated throughout the plane and her body. Then everything went black.

"Mayday, Mayday" was coming from the cockpit as the pilot tried to reach Air Command. The pilot tried to maneuver the plane without it's engines. He'd flown for over twenty years and never imagined being in this position. He was momentarily deeply saddened, not by the potential and likely loss of his life, but the hurt his four kids and wife would feel by his loss. How would they make it without him.

He was the sole breadwinner of his family. His heart ached to see his kids once more as he tried to maneuver the plane for a water landing. He longed to kiss his beautiful wife of twenty two years again and tell her he loved her. It was all too sad and there was nothing he could do. They were going down and fast. He felt the Plane trying to level off without doing it's death spiral into the ocean. His heart soared with the potential that he may be able to save them, then he realized he didn't have enough time. The ocean rushed towards him too fast, they weren't going to make it.

It wasn't enough.

That was the last thought that flashed in his mind before the plane crashed nose first into the ocean, breaking the cockpit glass and taking the pilot meandering into open ocean.

It wasn't enough.

# *ELEVEN*

EVERY MUSCLE IN ALLISON'S body hurt. From the pounding in her head to the stiffness in her legs, pain reverberated throughout every fiber of Allison's body. She felt like she was laying on nails. Nails that were set on fire upon which she was placed to cook. Maybe, she thought, she was being sacrificed on some kind of alter?

She was no virgin, so good luck on whatever ritual was being attempted. Everything burned, but it wasn't getting hotter, it was just a constant heat engulfing her entire body. Before she attempted to open her eyes, Allison tried to remember where she was. Nothing came. She opened her eyes, afraid of what she'd find on the other side. The blur of new sight was replaced by blue, deep blue as far as the eyes could see.

Still confused, Allison tried to sit up on her elbows, but the pain in her back shot through her like lightening and she fell back down. Her hands explored the earth she thought were nails and came up with sand. It started coming together. Sand and blue, she was on a beach.

What the hell was she doing on a beach?

She tried again to sit up, pushing through the pain, after all she was no wuss. Lush tropical vegetation greeted her to one side and the ocean the other. Large crashing waves collided with the sand. Allison sat there mesmerized by the ocean and the green of the jungle to the east. She realized she was on an island, there were no boats, and no one else that she could see.

It started in her hands, and moved to her teeth. Trembling. The realization that she was alone on what looked like an island without knowing how she got there and why she was there caused her body to shake uncontrollably. Panic threatened to consume her, so she bit her lip until the salty, metallic taste of blood hit her tongue. The sting of pain, temporarily got her to calm down.

She started to go through the things she did know, maybe that would jar her memory. Maybe this was all a dream, a nightmare and she had to find her way back to reality.

"My name is Allison Caine." The familiar sound of her voice calmed her so she continued.

"I am twenty-four years old. I was born in Nanuet, New York to Celeste and Thomas Caine. I was a cheerleader and played soccer in High school. I went to UGA and graduated with a degree in Accounting. I worked at a bookstore in college. "

Memories rushed through her mind, reminding her of who she was. The memories grounded her so she continued.

"My best friend is Samantha..We just bought a Condo together. We live in Atlanta, Georgia and I work for Abbotts, Glen and Notto PC. I've worked there for two years and my boss is Mr. Osmund...."

Little by little it came to her. " Mr. Osmund assigned me the Anderson deal and I went to the Cayman Islands to complete it. when I was there I ran into Bryson Anderson Jr. My one night stand and father of my unborn baby...."

At that moment, Allison wrapped her hands around her stomach and remembered. She was on the way with Bryson for some files. They were flying, she heard a boom then everything went dark.

A scream tried to escape from Allison, but her mouth and throat were so dry nothing came. All of her memories came back to her, and none of it mattered. Not the happiness of getting a job, or the anger of being left after a one night stand. What mattered was her baby. Her baby growing inside her.

But, was it still there? Was her baby still growing, still alive?

Panic once again engulfed Allison The fear of loss made her unable to think. She lifted the torn skirt and looked at her panties and legs. No blood. Good, that was good, but how long had she been there? What if the ocean water had washed away any signs. Allison pushed the thought out of her head. A fierce rush of protective instincts rushed Allison. She wanted her baby, and now she didn't know if she had it anymore.

"I didn't know you went to UGA, I went to Georgia Tech."

Allison screamed in fright as she pushed herself away from the sound.

At Allison's reaction, Bryson dropped the coconuts he had in his hands and ran towards her. For someone who was injured, she moved fast. He stopped short when he saw the fear on her face. She was in shock and he didn't want to make it worse.

When the plane went down, he'd initially blacked out, but came to pretty fast. They were lucky, the plane went down in the middle of the day so at least they weren't shrouded in total blackness of the ocean at night. As someone who took amateur flying lessons, Bryson knew his way around a private aircraft.

With blood flowing down his face from a gash on his forehead, Bryson fought his way to the door  to the inflatable raft. In the mangled aircraft,  Bryson looked up and he was looking at the sky. He realized the roof of the aircraft had cracked open and was floating somewhere in the Atlantic. Adrenaline fueled his movements as his mind and rational thinking took a back seat. Searing pain from the injuries on his head and legs didn't reach his brain. If they did, he didn't feel it.  He tried to make his way to the cockpit and saw there was no cockpit. Whatever happened when the plane went down, must have been devastating because the cockpit along with the pilot was gone.

The pilot Arnold McKenzie, he'd know since he was sixteen years old. A pang of loss gripped his heart and he sagged against a half standing wall. Dizziness made him almost fall but he held on to a chair that was still in place. He made his way back to his seat.  Seated beside him was

Allison, bloodied and bruised, but alive. He saw the gentle rise and fall of her chest.

Shutting off all emotion and pain, he threw the raft over the remaining walls of the aircraft into a calm ocean, making sure to have the string that connected him to the raft securely around his wrist. He gently unbuckled Allison from her seat, which was still intact and in place. Thank God he decided to opt for the upgraded plane package and didn't skimp like his mother said he should have. Life was priceless.

Bryson placed Allison gently into the crux of his chest. He moved slowly because at any moment, the floating aircraft could sink more rapidly and they would both be doomed. As he moved, water flowed into the ruined plane. He used his hands and wiped the blood pooling on her head, above her eyes and mouth away.

She looked so peaceful.

He placed his hands gently over her heart and a smile graced his lips as he felt her strong and steady heart beat.

"My fighter," he said to no one. He looked at her leg and saw that both her knees were bleeding, he just hoped they weren't broken. Carefully, he carried Allison out of the crashed aircraft and maneuvered her onto the raft. No easy task for a dizzy man who'd just gone though some major trauma carefully carrying a pregnant—hopefully-- only bruised woman. But he made it and they were safely in the raft.

Debris floated around them and he reached and took what he could put in the boat. The plane refrigerator, with four cans of coca-cola spilling out of it. The food cabinet with only candy and peanuts floating inside it and a navy blanket, torn and wet. He'd gathered these items and let the calm current of the ocean take them away.

The sting of the salty air against his wounds didn't distract Bryson from the shock and pain of floating away from the plane. As he got further and further away, he felt more and more alone. Alone and away from safety, because although the plane was wrecked and broken and was about to sink, it was familiar.

Floating in a yellow inflatable raft, in the middle of the Ocean with only an unconscious Allison, a hollow empty chasm opened in his chest. It may be the last time he ever saw anything remotely familiar. As he watched the plane disappear in the distance, he pondered if this was the last time he would see anything remotely safe.

Sailing on the Atlantic's current, Bryson knew they had to fend for themselves. It would be him, Allison and the child she was carrying. He didn't need a lot of time or a nervous breakdown to tell him that. If they were going to have any hope or chance of making it out of this alive, although he had no idea if that was even possible, it would be up to him.

He stared as Allison, confused tried to retreat from him. Hurt flashed across his face a second before he proceeded to coax her into calming down.

"Allison, It's me Bryson." The mistrust in her eyes did not recede.

"I figured I'd take you to my private island for a little R&R, a little wine and dine action. So whatdya' think?"

Bryson had his hands open gesturing around with a goofy smile on his face. The mistrust coming from Allison warped into a 'are you kidding me?' look that told Bryson he was getting through to her.

"Yeah, Isle de Bryson, or Isle Bryson, land of hunger, injury and aggravation. I'm still working on the catch phrase. I'm going to one day make it a cruise ship destination, I can see it now. 'Get stranded on Isle Bryson, once you get here, you'll never leave.' Get it?"

Bryson thought he saw a roll of her eyes. She remembered him.

"How are you? I went to hunt and gather."

Allison still didn't say anything, but Bryson could see she was starting to relax.

"Here, have some coconut water."

Bryson walked over to Allison, taking his time without making any sudden movements. He didn't want the progress he'd made with her to vanish. He knelt beside her and placed his hand behind her neck and gently guided her to drink from the coconut. She hesitated at first but when the first drop of sweet fresh liquid touched her lips, Allison started to gulp down the rest. She looked up at Bryson and their eyes met.

He saw appreciation and relief there. Relief of what, he didn't know. For the last two days he watched over Allison, took care of her and worried himself into a few gray hairs. He wanted something else, something more personal than relief and appreciation. He sat down next to her and opened the other coconut for her. She took it and nodded a thank you in response.

He wanted to hear her voice again. As she spoke to herself earlier, if felt great to hear someone, especially Allison's voice after the absence of human sounds for the past few days. He wanted to hear it again.

"So when were you going to tell me you were having my baby?"

Startled, Allison stared at Bryson for what seemed liked an interminably amount of time.

"I don't know. Maybe if you were there when I woke up the next morning--."

"There was no way you could have know you were pregnant then."

"There was also no way I'd know you were a total jerk then either?"

"Well now you know, so when were you going to tell me you were having my baby?"

"Bryson, I'm having your baby."

# *TWELVE*

ALLISON COULDN'T BELIEVE SHE just said that out loud to Bryson. Ugh! What was she thinking? But he'd heard her. Where the hell were they anyway.

"Where are we?"

"I don't know exactly, I don't exactly have my GPS on me to tell you."

Allison rolled her eyes and looked away. Where ever they were, this was no good.

"Is there anyone else here?"

"As far as I can see....no."

That seemed so final. No one, just Bryson. The panic started again.

"How are we going to get out of here?"

Bryson studied Allison's face, becoming more serious as the seconds passed. The waves seemed far away and the air around them was still, and quiet.

"I don't know."

Tears welled up and released down her cheeks.

Allison began to cry. She didn't know why she was crying exactly. Was it the throbbing pain throughout her body? The fear for her baby? The isolation of being on a deserted island or the thought that this could be the last place she sees before she dies? The entire calamity was too much, too much to handle.

Her crying was becoming uncontrollable. Bryson, stuck in place looked surprised, then he scooted over to her and put his hand around her shoulders. Glad for the contact and comfort, Allison turned her head into Bryson's chest and sighed.

The reality started setting in. They were here by themselves. All the while Bryson absent-mindedly rubbed Allison's arm up and down whispering soothing reassurances to her. They stayed like that until the tide started to come in. Long enough for the sun to begin to fall behind the horizon. The sand, water and sky lit up with brilliant hues of reds, yellows and oranges and the waves calmed to a whisper.

*If this wasn't the last place I'd see*, she thought *it would be perfect*.

She grieved but was ready to put away grieving and get down to business.

"So What do we do now?" Bryson sighed and stared towards the sea.

"First, let me get the fire going."

He reluctantly let Allison go and went to start a fire. In theory, that was easier said than done. While Allison was unconscious, Bryson was busy gathering wood and sticks which he'd place in a nice pile a few feet away. He seen it done in movies as well as on TV many times.

*How hard could it be?* He thought. *You rub two sticks together and wha-la, flaming fire.*

Movies and real life... totally different.

After trying to rub two sticks together for what seemed like forever, Bryson stood up and looked over at Allison.

He saw her face, sitting there beautifully waiting and counting on him to make it happen. He couldn't give up now. He knew at that moment more than any, in his what was looking to be a very short life, what his mission in life was. To provide for Allison Caine.

His pampered life was gone.

Out here he was Bryson, period. No name was going to help him. No amount of money was going to buy him favor. Only his knowledge and will to survive was currency. Not only survive for his sake, but for Allison's also. She needed him more than ever, and he would not fail.

Who would she have if not him. Once again he went at it, rubbing those damn sticks together until one broke. He threw them down frustrated. How was he going to do this? He refused to go out like this, night was coming and he knew it was going to get cold. The previous two nights were a warm up for what he felt was going to be cold. He walked out toward the water, kicking sand every which way. Then,

"Bryson," a whisper with a hint of laughter came to his ear. "Bryson," he turned, defeated to see Allison standing there.

"What? I'm trying to start a fire here."

"By kicking sand? Last time I checked that's not how it's done."

How did Allison have the ability to illicit such annoyance in him. Just when he was going all Alpha Male, she goes and ruins it.

"Would you like to try, seeing as you know so much, fire starter."

As if by magic, Allison produced an orange Bic lighter.

"You could always try this."

Astonished, Bryson looked incredulously at Allison.

"Where did you get this? Did you have this all along."

"No I didn't have it all along, I found it poking me in the side, I looked down and it was buried in the sand under me."

He thanked God that he decided to quit smoking next week. It must have fell off him somehow.

"What is a good girl like you doing with a lighter?"

"Don't let the good looks fool you, The only thing good about me is my lovin "

With a wicked smile, Allison turned and walked back to where she was sitting.

His Allison was back.

With a nice roaring fire started, Bryson sat beside Allison and tucked her in under his arms. He used his right hand to slowly caress the thick curls falling all around her face.

"How are you doing?" He moved his left hand down to her stomach and gently patted. With a heavy sigh, she replied, "I don't know how I'm doing. I'm a little stunned."

"It makes sense to be. This was a pretty dramatic thing we went through."

"How long has it been? What day is it?"

"You've been sleeping for a day and a half."

With a wry smile, Allison said "sleeping"?

"Sleeping, passed out, near death, whats the difference," said Bryson with a small smirk.

"Well, I'm alright now, I just don't know if my …"

"If what?"

"Nothing."

A long silence passed between them. The only sound was the wind and ocean.

This was scary. What were they going to do. How long could they stay like this? That unspoken question weighed on the the minds of both Bryson and Allison.

"What do you think happened?" asked Allison

"I don't know, maybe when we get out of here, we'll find out. But who knows, the plane is at the bottom of the ocean, I doubt we'll ever know what happened, exactly."

"When we get out of here? You seem very sure of that."

"You haven't met my parents, they will search this entire planet inch by inch until they find me."

With a playful smile Allison said, "What are they going to do when they find me? Throw me back?"

Bryson's face hardened with intensity and started at Allison. "I will never lose you again. Nothing will make me throw you anywhere except up against one of those palm trees while I--"

"Don't do that."

"Don't do what?"

"What ever that was."

"What ever what was?"

"That suave, sexy thing you do when you are trying to seduce me, but it's not going to work."

"Oh sure, that thing. Well I wasn't trying to seduce you, I was just telling it like it is."

"Paaleeezzze."

"I'm serious, I'm just keeping it real."

"Real corny."

"When I had you up against the wall in my Penthouse, I didn't hear you saying nothing 'bout corny."

"Whatever, that was when I was an impressionable girl, now, my dear Bryson I am a hardened experienced single pregnant woman."

What a way to crash and burn the mood.

The playfulness of the conversation dissipated into the night air. Both Bryson and Allison retreated from each other a little and everything became oh so very awkward.

Frustrated and fed up with not talking about their baby, Bryson jumped right in.

"We are here together now, I don't know how long we'll have, so we need to figure out what we're going to do."

"I don't want to--"

"You can't keep running away from this Allison, you have to deal with it."

"How dare you tell me I have to deal with it, I'm dealing with it everyday. You are the one that is not dealing with it."

"Sorry, I didn't mean that. But I am trying to, but you won't let me."

"Poor Bryson, finally didn't get something he wanted."

He interrupted her taunting and said, "Stop it, stop it right now.!"

"Or what?" A defiant hold to her face.

"Don't test me Allison, I'm not one to play with."

"What are you going to do, because of you we are stuck in the middle of God-knows-where. I'm hurt and hungry, and I don't know if I'll live to see myself get off this island. Don't test you. Shove it, okay."

"You know what your problem is, you're angry at the

world--"

"No, I'm angry at you"

"--and you have to realize--"

"Who are you, Dr. Phil? I don't need your diagnosis."

"That I want to be a family--"

"A whaaat?"

"...and I think we can do it, we can work it out together like a team.

"You have got to be kidding me. You go from dropping me after a one night stand to wanting a family? If there was anyone else here I would ask them how absurd that sounds. Oh Yeah, I forgot, We're stranded!"

"It makes sense though doesn't it."

"Ah...no it doesn't I don't want a family with you--"

"Then what do you want Allison, look me in the eye and tell me what it is you want."

Bryson moved and stood right in front of Allison and waited.

Overwhelmed and surprised by the directness of the question Allison looked away. Quite frankly, she never thought about what she actually wanted, she only concentrated on what was expected of her. What her Mother wanted for her, What her Dad expected of her, what someone of her upbringing should be doing. She followed the manual of life and only concentrated on getting to the next step, the next promotion, the next trophy for her mantel. What she wanted never occurred to her.

"I-I don't know what I want."

Bryson looked as taken aback as Allison felt.

"Maybe I can help you figure it out."

"How do you plan on doing that?"

"I have my ways."

"Remember this is what I want not what you want."

"Yeah, I know, I know but--"

"Why did you leave me in that hotel room...alone?"

Uncomfortable, Bryson got up and started pacing back and forth. His toes gripping and releasing the sand.

"I don't know, it was a moment of weakness I guess."

"You guess?! Are we being honest with each other here or are we just jerking off?"

"I don't know what happened. I panicked and then when I calmed down and came back you were gone. I was so happy when I saw you a few days ago." When he arrived back at the room and Allison was no where to be found, a sense of loss washed over him, but also a sense of relief. Although he didn't like it, things took care of themselves, He didn't have to make the heart wrenching choices, until now.

"You panicked? Over what?"

"I don't want to talk about this anymore."

"Tough titties. Why did you leave me?"

There was so much loaded in that question. Allison need to justify the rejection that bubbled in her blood. She'd given him her, purely her, and he rejected it. Bryson recognized this was the reason she was so angry with him, and he needed not mess up his answer.

He wanted to, but he couldn't... but he had to. With every change in decision, Bryson changed the direction he was walking in on the sand, eventually walking around in a circle.

"Bryson...Bryson, can you please stop walking around in a circle, you are causing a tornado."

"You are a funny one aren't you."

"I try, now answer the question."

"I didn't want it to get too serious with you."

"Why did you think we would get serious. Not leaving someone alone in the bed after you've had your way with them is a far cry from a possible relationship. Who said I wanted a relationship anyway?"

"Oh all you women want a relationship."

"Hey Bryson, jump down from that high horse will ya?"

"It's true, that is what you all want."

"I resent that, so why did you allegedly come back?"

"Allegedly?"

"It's not proven."

"Are you calling me a liar now?"

"I don't know yet, go on."

"Go on what?"

"Why did you come back?"

"Because I really liked you. I've had women all around the world and no one has ever made me feel the way you do."

"I don't know, I watch enough Law and Order to know that I'm missing something. There is something you are not telling me. It's just not a complete story."

"TV is different from real life," said Bryson.

"Sometimes, sometimes not. Look Bryson, tell me the truth. There is no one else around, no one to hear but me. Little ole' me. I can't hurt you, how bad could it be? There is something inside me that just wants to know why. Why after such a great night, after I opened myself to you, after I trusted you, why would you leave me. I remember our night together, you didn't seem concerned about how serious our 'relationship' was getting. You were loving it as I remember. That night, you were not an unsure man."

"How do you know? What, are you an expert on men?" He was getting defensive. He didn't want to talk about it.

"I know what I feel and something is wrong."

"I gotta go find some more firewood."

Bryson walked towards the edge of the forest to gather more wood.

*Why did she have to push so hard*, thought Bryson. *Why couldn't she just leave it alone.*

Scared, she'd said, he wasn't scared, he just wanted to keep his private reasons to himself, hence the term private. But how did he expect to get through to Allison if she didn't know the whole truth. How was he going to get her to talk about their possible future. Throwing down the few pieces of firewood he had in his hands, Bryson stomped back to where Allison was sitting down and said,

"I didn't want us to get serious because I was engaged to be married."

# *THIRTEEN*

"YOU WERE WHAT?!" SAID Allison, kneeling on her knees to get up.

She'd had it. She moved closer to him with a menacing look on her face. A woman on the prowl and Bryson was her prey. Allison never took well to betrayal.

"You are here talking about family and us and I almost believed you, all the while you belong to someone else. Once again you fool little ole' me." Allison started talking to herself more than she was talking to Bryson although with every word, she inched closer to him with two fists at her side.

"Listen--"

"There is nothing I want to hear from you. You got that? Nothing." Speaking to herself again

"Why am I so stupid. You think I'd learn, but no, hard headed Allison just won't--"

"It's not like that--"

"Don't interrupt me when I'm talking to myself."

"Ally its not as bad as it seems really. I--"

"HA!" her head going back as she laughed.

"Save it for your Wife." Allison rushed towards Bryson. She pounded on his chest as hard as she could. She was met with a rock hard chest. There was no give under her fists. He finally reached for Allison's hands to stop the assault.

"With red tear filled eyes Allison looked at Bryson and asked. "What did I ever do to you?"

"You gave me some of the best time of my life and a potential family, that's what you did to me. Ally," He took her chin and raised it to meet her eyes.

"I really am sorry. I'm sorry for this whole thing, but I'm not lying, I want you. I do want a life with you."

Allison left his grip and went back to where she was sitting. She sat with her knees pushing against her chest and stared out at the waves without saying anything. Bryson came to sit next to her and he felt good she didn't push him away. They stayed that way for a long time, not saying anything, just staring out at the water, the stars and the moon.

Allison let out a defeated breath and turned to face Bryson.

"I broke off the engagement you know." He said.

Allison didn't say anything. She just stared at Bryson.

"Yeah, it's over, done with. Just for the record, it wasn't a love thing, you know, the marriage. "

Allison stared.

"It was kind of a business relationship. Her parents are very good friends with my parents as well as business partners. We had an exploratory committee research me running for public office and the results were, I had to get married. Everyone thought that would give my campaign a better chance."

Bryson paused.

"I've known her almost all my life, our parents are close so it was a natural fit. I know, I know what you're thinking. What does that have to do with anything?"

Still, Allison just stared.

" I've made my money. Now I want to give back. I can't be bribed because I have more money that I could spend in twenty lifetimes so I thought it would be a good fit. Plus I think Lauren always fancied me to an extent. It wasn't a bad deal for either of us so I went with it. But it wasn't love.

"So you used me, with all intensions to leave me."

"It wasn't like that and you know it. I had no 'intensions' everything happened naturally. I didn't plan a thing. I think we've fought enough for the day don't you? I've got some stuff to eat."

Bryson reached over and retrieved a coconut from beside him and cut it open with his pocket knife. Then he produced three small bags of peanuts to go with it. At the sight of real food albeit snack food, Allison cheered up. With all the excitement of the day, Allison felt exhausted.

Relaying this to Bryson bought a blanket for Allison to sleep with. The last thing she saw before she went to sleep was Bryson tucking her in.

## *FOURTEEN*

NICOLAS STEVENSON PUSHED THE heavy mahogany door that led into his Mother in law's Antoinette's study open. As soon as she saw him enter, she ran to him and broke down in tears.

"Oh Nick. They found the plane, but they haven't found your brother yet." Marsha his wife and Antoinette's daughter did everything in her power to make her husband feel accepted into the Anderson clan. Her mother was on line, but she was the only one.

She openly sobbed in his arms. She'd been crying in her husbands arms for the last two days. She wanted a new shoulder to cry on.

"It's alright Mom, he'll be okay. We'll find him."

"What if...." Antoinette broke into another round of uncontrollable sobs.

This was not the woman Nick knew. Antoinette was a fierce lioness to her husband's King of the Jungle persona. Together they were able to grow a loan from her dad into a multi billion dollar empire. All the money and diamonds meant nothing especially when it came to her kids. Bryson Jr. and Marsha and by extension Nick.

Antoinette reached up and touched the cheeks of her Son in Law. "I love you dearly. You mean so much to me."

"I know that Mom." Nick's parents were not alive and Antoinette had always tried to play the part.

"I just want you to know, because you never know what tomorrow or even today will bring."

"Does anyone know what happened?" asked Nick.

"They recovered the plane and they are going to investigate what happened."

"What about the sale of Sun-splash resorts. We're going to have to figure out how to handle it."

"I can't think about that right now," screamed Antoinette.

"Mother, I know you are upset, but the world still turns although your beloved Bryson is not here. There is a breach of contract clause in the contract that if it is not closed within seventy-two hours, the deal goes bust. We could lose millions."

"I don't care about the money, I don't care about the resort. I don't--"

"Nick is right Antoinette," said Bryson's father.

"Business is business and we do not want our competitors to think we are weak because we are going through some family difficulties."

"Family difficulties? This is not a family difficulty, this is a life and death situation--"

"Be that as it may, we must still function. We cannot give up on living and performing the duties entrusted upon us."

With a whirl, Antoinette picked up her bag and headed for the door.

"You can't go out that way, there are nothing but reporters out there."

She turned and went to the back door of the study.

"You two can continue to pretend that nothing is wrong, and nothing is happening, my son is missing and I am going to do what I can to get him back. Before the door closed they heard "in what ever state he's in."

With the two of them there, Bryson senior turned to his son in law and said,

"I've always had high hopes for you. My daughter didn't want in on my business. She was content to coddle you all day and have your babies. Plus, I don't do well with outsiders having the inside track on what's going on."

That hurt Nick tremendously. He'd been trying to get "in" since the day he married his daughter.

"I don't know what's going to come of this, but I'm a man that hopes for the best, and plans for the worse."

Bryson senior moved to the heavy mahogany desk draw and pulled out a cuban cigar. He cut the end off and lit it. Puffing on the cigar created a strong tobacco smell throughout the room, he gazed at Nick through the smoke, "Can you step in if needed? You've never had a head for my business. It never suited you."

"Is that why Bryson was the one picked to run for office. I'm the one that's married with children, not him."

A momentary flash of surprise crossed Bryson seniors face. It happened so fast, if you didn't know him, you would have missed it.

"I hope you would have known, there is more to public office than your marital status. Bryson truly wants to do this, you just want to be famous."

The more Bryson Sr. thought about it, the more perturbed he became.

"...and never forget for a second, he is my only Son, and I will do any and everything for him."

"I didn't mean anything by it. It's just that I know I can run, if you give me a chance."

"We'll, see what happens. You need to be able to read people, their strengths and weaknesses. That's what's gotten this family to where it is today. You need to know when to attack, and when to retreat." Puffing on the cigar once again then admiring the handiwork of the craftsmanship of the cigar, Bryson senior said, "You have never been able to do that, and you end up attacking when you should retreat and retreating when you should attack."

Nick had heard enough. This was nothing new. Yeah yeah yeah, you're a loser, yeah yeah yeah, you need to be more like Bryson Jr., yadda yadda yadda. Yeah, well whose at the bottom of the Atlantic ocean right now and who isn't?

"Look, I'm going to be late for my appointment if I stay any longer," said Nick.

"It can wait. Here is your opportunity to turn back your reputation. I want you to handle the Sun-splash resort deal. You will have to meet up with Deval and make sure everyone is on the same page. I need you to do this right. All you have to do is go in as a representative for the family and sign the paperwork."

It was all coming together nicely.

"Father, I will not let you down." Bryson flinched at how Nick referred to him. Nick knew it bothered him, but he wanted to make the old man a little uncomfortable. Nick turned and walked out the door with the reporters on the other side.

He didn't realize Bryson Sr. saw the small smirk that appeared on his face as he left the room.

Bryson Senior chalked it up to the fact that Nick was given another chance to get it right. But something was forming at the pit of his stomach that told him, this was going to go from bad, to worse.

Pulling out a bottle of Jack Daniels to go with his cigar, Bryson senior wondered about his daughters husband. Was it too easy for them? Did he help them out too much? Nick was a man, and as a man, there was no room for mistakes, no room for carelessness. Having to make it on his own, he learned some of the most valuable lessons during some of his hardest times. Because he was successful, his children didn't have to go through what he had to and in turn missed out on some life saving lessons.

Taking a drink of whisky, Bryson Senior enjoyed the burn of the alcohol going down his throat. Well, he did the best he could, if it wasn't enough, there was nothing he could do about it now. He finished the drink with one gulp and reached for the bottle.

Millie, his assistant, buzzed in on the office phone located on his desk next to the whisky bottle.

"Mr. Anderson, there is a Mr. Caine on the phone for you."

"Millie, I said no calls."

"He said he's the father of Allison Caine."

"I don't care if it's the King of Monaco, no calls." After a long pause, Millie said, "He's the father of Allison Caine Sir, the woman who was on the plane with Bryson."

Closing his eyes, Bryson senior rubbed them until they too burned. He poured himself another drink and reached for the phone.

"Thank you Millie. I'll take it."

## *FIFTEEN*

ALLISON WOKE UP WITH the light from the sun nudging and pushing her lids open. She reached to her side and realized she was alone...again.

"Dammit!"

He'd left her again. "Ugh!" she moaned and got up. Her bones still ached but it felt better to stretch them than stay laying on the hot sand. She looked left, nothing but sand greeted her. She looked to her right, sand again.

"Did I scare you so much again you decided to take your chance in the ocean?" Yelled Allison at the top of her lungs. She didn't believe what she was saying because she didn't start to panic.

"Will you pipe down, you'll attract the wild animals."

"Huh?" Allison was momentarily frozen with fear.

"What wild animals?"

"Me."

Despite herself, Allison smiled. "Where were you? Once again I woke up after sleeping with you, and found you gone."

"Look, you are not going to hold that over my head forever are you? I told you I came back, and you were gone. Every time I go to the bathroom, I will not come back to you questioning me like I'm on probation."

"Maybe you are."

"Why would I be? I know you were hurt but--"

"But nothing." Allison limped over to him stopping barely an inch from his face.

"Yes you hurt me, and lied to me. If I don't get over it on your schedule, that's too bad. I will hold this against you as long as I so well please, and you are not going to tell me differently."

The fire in her eyes made Bryson's heart pump a little harder and a little faster. He loved when she burst with emotion like this. He reached out and put his hand behind her neck, drew her into him and kissed her deep, strong and confident.

He felt her relax into him and join in the dance of their tongues. He'd wanted to do this for months. He missed the soft and sexy curve of her body, the sweet smell of her skin. At that moment he wanted inside of her, see if she would respond to him. Lost in the moment, Bryson didn't see Allison's hand speeding towards his face and colliding with it. That broke the connection and the buzz he was building.

"Don't think about doing that again."

"Come on, you loved it," said Bryson rubbing his face.

"In your dreams."

"I know that, but you loved it just now too."

"We are not friends Bryson." He saw her twist her face as she said his name. "Let's try to figure out what we are going to do until we're rescued."

"And then?"

"We'll go our separate ways. The same way you left me."

"Will you get over that already. I told you I was on the way back."

"Yeah but-"

"Plus, you forgot one little detail, no, a big detail, you are carrying my child." He saw her tense and look away.

"Do we have anything to eat, my stomach is growling. I'm starving."

Bryson looked at her for a long time before he said.

"You are not going to be able to avoid this for long. We hash this out after we eat."

"What are we going to eat."

"Well, I have good news and bad news, which one do you want to hear first."

"The good news."

I know where we are. We were only a few miles from the island when the plane went down. I don't know if you are a religious person, but either through the help of GOD or luck, the tide took us to the island."

"Really? What's here."

"My villa. It's the only property on the island as well as a few water falls, medicine, food water, beds you name it. We will be stranded in style."

"Can we call anyone?"

"No, there is only cell phone coverage and we have no cell phone."

"Don't you have a backup at the villa."

"Haven't anyone told you not to look a gift horse in the mouth?"

"Ok, OK you're right. I'm happy I won't have to sleep on the sand again tonight. Wait a minute, why don't I see it, where is this villa?"

"That's the bad news. It's on the other side of the island."

"Uh oh! How far is that?" As if Allison's knee and ankles heard her inquiry, they started to hurt.

"It's only about three miles if we walk around the island instead of walking through the mini jungle and up through the quasi mountains."

"Mountains?"

"Look around you."

Allison hadn't noticed the rolling lush green hills that rose internally on the island.

"Oh." This was good news, but she didn't think she could make it. Her feet hurt and she was unstable, hungry and hot with sand finding it's way into all her crevaces. She was uncomfortable everywhere.

"I-I don't know--" It hurt her to admit to herself and him she couldn't do it.

"Maybe if we go slow." She tried again. She could bear it, but what amount of stress would it cause on the little one growing inside of her. Well, she still hoped it was still growing inside of her. Swallowing her pride she said, "I don't know if I can make it right now, to the Villa."

Without warning, Bryson scooped her up into his arms and said, "I told you kitten, I got you." His words took her back to one of the best times in her life. She could never deny her feelings for him, or the feelings he was giving off in droves. He may have hurt her, but their time two months ago, meant something, she knew as much as she knew water was wet, he meant what he said. But she couldn't give into him again like she did before. Looking into his golden eyes, she refused to be caught up in him like she had before.

"Thank you." said Allison.

"I need you to carry the bag, and I'll carry you. Deal?"

"Deal."

He put her down and instructed her to get on his back, which she did slowly and cautiously. He gave her the bag with the cokes and the rest of the few items he retrieved from the plane and started out towards the villa.

Bryson was hot, hungry and tired from his early morning rise and trek across the island and back. By himself he was able to do it in no time, running on the adrenaline of joy he felt for being where he was. This could have been a lot worse.

He looked at the sky and noticed an ominous cloud miles to the south of them. It could have gotten very bad. But he wasn't going to dwell on that now. He had his family on his back, literally, and he felt great that he was able to get them to safety. It didn't matter how tired he was or how his back, and knees ached. He would get Allison to the villa safe, feed her and have her relax in a soft bed.

Bryson wasn't a religious man, but he found God fast as he laid and stared at the stars last night. Prayer, the last refuge of a scoundrel. He made promises he hoped he could keep last night. He got his reprieve, their chance of surviving went from 5% to 95%, it was now his turn to satisfy his side of the bargain.

He wasn't thinking of that now, he was filled with such joy and masculine pride that he, Bryson Daniel Anderson Jr. was being the man that circumstances called for. He wasn't using his vast bank account or his family connections to get things done. It was man against nature and hopefully, he would win. At least until they were found.

The adrenaline took Bryson but so far with Allison on his back. He walked around the island and didn't trek into the jungles until the last possible moment. At first the semi even ground of the sand had him going at a steady pace, but after an hour with an extra hundred plus pounds on his back, he had to slow down. The hot sun punishing their backs and body slowed him down even more.

They'd stop for something to drink twice already at the urging of Allison. She saw he was tired but wouldn't rest on his own.

She knew if she told him she needed it, he would do it. Allison reveled in her position. She felt safe and cared for. It felt good.

Looking up after an additional two hours of walking, Bryson stopped and Allison looked up. They'd reached the walkway of the expansive villa. It greeted them with towering walls and huge windows. The villa was a mansion. Allison grew up in a three bedroom two bathroom house with a garage and a back yard. This villa looked like they could fit five of her houses in it. It was beautiful and stunning.

Vibrant blood red flowers were planted all around with yellow lilies intertwining the landscape. Whoever designed the landscaping was going for tropical paradise. Tropical multi colored birds flew around them, butterflies flew around the flowers and the ocean crashed behind it all.

Allison shifted on his back, preparing herself to get down, but Bryson started walking again.

"I can walk from here," said Allison

"We are not there yet."

He walked until he opened the massive dark wood door and let her down over the threshold. No need for a key, the only way on or off the island was through a plane or boat. There was no landing strip, but the planes they used were the small ones that landed in water and a raft was taken to the shore.

Inside was breathtaking. Marble floors lead to windows extending from the floor to ceiling that outlined the massive and imposing blue ocean. Awed, Allison walked over to the window and stared at the ocean. The vastness of it in ever direction made her tremble. The ocean was not a friendly place. It could be violent and dangerous.

Recently, she was out in it, in the ocean after a plane came crashing down.

She could have been dead.

That was the first time she'd allowed herself to think that. She instinctively reached for her stomach. Her baby could be lost to the violent ocean. The possibility of that had her reeling. No, she didn't want to become a mother now, she had plans. But the idea of the life maturing inside of her as well as her near death spiral into the deep blue ocean, had her protective maternal instincts kicking in.

Bryson put his hand on her shoulder which startled her. She was so lost in thought, she forgot he was there.

"Let me show you around." He took her hand and led her to the right of where they came.

"Here is the kitchen," said Bryson as he swept his hand across the massive kitchen. They were moving fast so Allison didn't get a chance to take it all in.

"Here is a sitting room, and a bathroom over here, and here is your room."

Allison walked in and saw the large bed in front of her with lilly white and gold bedding. The bed was slanted towards the window of the ocean. Without thinking she went to the bed and collapsed onto it. A deep moan left her mouth.

"It's so soft." The pillow top mattress attempted to massage all her aches away. He walked in and showed her the connected bathroom.

"Here is the bathroom and if you look in the closet you'll see some clothes in there that should fit you."

"Whose clothes are they?"

"Does it matter, you don't have any other option." He had a point.

"I still want to know."

"It's usually for guests. Lauren usually stayed here when she came. But the clothes are pretty generic. Although I know she's worn some." Oh come on! but she didn't say that. She guessed Lauren must be his ex-fiance.

"Oh."

"Yeah well, after you shower, and relax, meet me in the kitchen and I'll prepare us something to eat."

"Are you going to cook?" asked Allison with skepticism touching every word.

"Who else? What, don't you think I can cook?"

"I figured you were just a spoiled rich boy who got everything done for him and didn't know how to do anything for yourself," said Allison.

"That would be Rich Man, I am no boy.

"Sorry...Rich man who got everything done for him and didn't know how to do anything for yourself."

"Once again you are wrong? I know how to cook very well. I was always a little paranoid so I learned."

"Paranoid?"

"Yes, Paranoid. When your parents have as much money as mine do, it pays to be cautious."

"Maybe you think you are too important."

"Just get dressed, dinner will be ready when you are ready." He turned and left the room.

The warm shower and subsequent nap Allison took, removed years from her body and face. She walked into the gourmet kitchen relaxed and refreshed, great. Her skin had a glow and Bryson noticed the yellow sundress she wore fit her perfectly, her just washed her hair made the curls bounce around as she walked.

"It smells great in here. What are you making."

It was three hours since they'd gotten to the villa and Bryson was hard at work. He also showered and smelled like cool breezes and coconut. That must be his body wash. He wore dark brown shorts loosely fitted and a close fitted white t-shirt.

"Stir fry vegetables with chicken and yellow rice."

"That sounds great."

"Get the dishes from there and set the table." He pointed her in the direction he wanted her to go. As he watched her comply he said, "I love it when a woman does what I tell her to do."

Allison almost pulled out her girl power badge to do a citizens arrest when she recognized the teasing in his voice.

"Don't you ever get tired of hearing yourself talk."

"Oh, all the time, but that's no reason for me to stop, is it?"

Allison methodically set the table, relaxing in the mundane task. A sense of normalcy returned to her demeanor. The last time she set the table, she was at her parents house. A pang of pain seized her heart and she had to hold on to the solid table for balance.

"What just happened?" asked Bryson running over and steadying her.

"I just thought about my Mom and Dad. They are probably on their way to my hotel as we speak, if they are not there already."

Bryson nodded knowingly and listened as she continued.

"It hurts me so much to think what they must be going through right now, not knowing what is happening with me."

Alli reached for her stomach out of reflex as she imagined dealing with the loss of a child.

"Isn't there any way to get word Bryson?" The pleading made Bryson stand up and rub his hands through his hair.

"I'll figure something out. Tell me about them. What's their names? They are my child's grandparents I would like to know more about them."

Allison tightened up and stopped talking.

"Look, this has to be dealt with period. The longer you put it off, the harder it will be. You can't wish this away."

"I know, I know," said Allison walking over to the refrigerator and pulling out the cranberry juice she saw. She knew she had to face this. Why she didn't want to, she wasn't totally sure. She never planned on talking about this with him, regardless if she should or shouldn't. She hadn't made the decision to, and now she was pushed into it.

Allison did not wing it very well.

"We don't know if I'm still pregnant."

"You know, that never occurred to me. Not pregnant? Why not just hit me over the head with a boulder. Anyway, you might be and that's enough reason."

For a second there, Bryson looked lost, like he didn't know what he was doing, or where he was. He calmed himself down, and served dinner.

"Now what?" asked Allison. The smooth and deep chuckle that she heard across the table bought a small smile to her face.

"We eat, that's what." After a few bites Bryson tried again.

"What's your parents name?"

'Thomas and Celeste Caine."

"I take it you guys have a good relationship?"

"Yeah we do. They've done everything they could have to give me a good education, and they still help me out to this day. They had very high hopes for me."

"Had?"

"Once they find out I've gone and gotten myself knocked up, it's going to devastate them."

"Why? It's not like you're a teenager."

"No, but this was not part of the plan. I was suppose to go to college, become a lawyer, get married, THEN have babies. Currently I'm not doing any of that. I hope they don't think they wasted their money on me. Do you know how much twelve years of private school and four years of college costs?"

"You can't think they're worried about the money are you? I mean you are their daughter, I'm sure they want you to be happy."

"Happy and successful. This," said Allison waving her hand up and down her body, "is not successful."

"It depends on your definition of success."

"Really, success is success. I bet you consider yourself successful."

"I used to, until I found out that you were pregnant."

"Huh?"

'Look, I have money--"

"That's an understatement--"

"...and many other things. I know a lot of people and have had my share of beautiful women all over the world--"

"Ok."

"I never thought I wanted a family before. It was for old people, and I wasn't old. The many powerful men I am surrounded with are all married, but they all have multiple affairs with women all over the world. That always seemed too much work for me. I tried it, it's not all it's cracked up to be."

"Yeah right."

"No really. You have to remember all the different quirks of each woman, you have to constantly buy them things to keep them interested, and they can become a hassle. Next thing you know, you end up hiding and living under a guise of quasi-secrecy. I'd rather do better things with my time."

"There are worse things to have to do--."

"And I started to see there are better things to do. I mean, after all the money, and women and things--"

"That sounds like a torturous existence--"

"What does it all mean? I want more, more meaning, more purpose, other than to collect money. When I heard you were pregnant with my baby, It felt like a breath of fresh air."

"When DID you find out I was pregnant?"

"The night of the banquet," said Bryson picking up their dishes as he spoke and depositing them in the dishwasher.

"That long. Oh God, I am so embarrassed right now. You knew that whole time? Why didn't you just say it?"

"Because I wanted *you* to tell me, which I see you had no intention of."

"That's because I didn't want you to know. I was going to give the baby up for adoption and get on with my life."

"But it's not only your life--"

"I never said I was perfect. I don't always do everything that's right. I just wanted it all to go away. I figured if I didn't say anything, it wouldn't be real."

He walked over to Allison and hugged her from behind while she sat in her chair.

"It is real, and its one of the most wonderful things that has ever happened to me." Allison didn't know why, but that statement pleased her beyond belief. She tried to suppress the huge smile that slowly graced her face, but she couldn't help it.

"Alli, kitten, I want to make this work."

"Work how?"

"I want us to be a family."

"This is all happening too fast."

"Sorry kitten, what's done is done. You are with child. You can't step back now."

"What are you in the 18th century? With child?"

"Knocked up, pregnant, with child it all means the same thing. You are having my baby... you are having my baby," said Bryson in a sing song voice. That got a laugh out of Allison.

"You are enjoying this way too much. Did you forget we are stranded here, your plane blew up and we don't know why or what happened. Planes don't just blow up. Plus we don't know how long we are going to be marooned here."

"Thanks for bringing that all up, for a moment I'd forgotten about all of that. I don't play games or beat around the bush. I don't have to. I'm not afraid to speak my mind. Before you change the subject. I want you to have no doubt in your mind that I'm in love with you."

"WHAT? How can I believe that. How could you love me."

Allison thought she loved him, but she didn't trust her emotions. She thought it was because she was carrying his baby. Maybe that had something to do with her overwhelming connection to Bryson. She sure as heck wasn't going to trust his words of love.

"I know because when I'm around you, my heart is happy. I'm calmed and I get this goofy smile on my face. That is, when you are not driving me mad. I know I love you because you are one of the only people who can drive me insane. You can push my buttons like no one has ever done. I know I love you because I would do anything *for* you, and anything *with* you. I know I love you because you make me stronger. I love you because I want the rest of my life to be about making you smile."

Wow. She didn't see that coming.

"But--"

"But nothing." Bryson reduced the space between them and raised her chin so she could look at him. "You are my everything Alli, and if I have to work every day for the rest of my life proving it to you, I will."

He stared in her deep brown eyes and watched her objections shatter. The current flowing between them was tinged with overwhelming love, and fear. He bore into her soul with his eyes and lowered his mouth to hers. Electricity passed from one to the other as Bryson pulled Allison close.

She wrapped her hands around his neck and pulled at his short locs while savoring every moment of their touch. Their tongues did at once a sweet dance of love, then migrated to greedy lust. Bryson moved to Alli's neck, marking her with his lips as he tasted her body. He felt home. It felt so right, it was scary. His hands found it's way under her dress. He caressed and squeezed his way up and down her soft curvy body. Stopping to show love at her breasts, nipples and her round ass. She matched him running her hands up his hard body. He reached under her dress and realized she wasn't wearing any panties.

"Where are your panties?" he asked surprised.

"I didn't have any." Touching her naked skin under her dress brought out a low growl from him.

He continued to explore her body as he kissed her, trying to take away her fear at the same time. He reached between her legs and felt her arousal on his fingers. Enjoying Allison's soft silky skin, Bryson took one finger and slipped it inside her. The moan Allison released was welcomed as he doubled the amount of fingers caressing her. He teased her with his fingers going in and out, round and round.

"Wow...that's awesome," whispered Allison into his closest ear."

Her body responded by coating his fingers with her thick cream. Taking his fingers out of her, he looked at her while he sucked his fingers.

"You taste better than anything I've ever cooked."

Allison's knees got weak. He lifted her up and put her on the table, with a surprised squeak from her. He kept surprising her at every turn. It felt great to relax into the moment. Not worry about protocol or have to plan anything beyond the next second. She surrendered to his hands.

He flipped her dress up, and went to work kissing her other lips. He licked and sucked, gently at first then more aggressively. Like all he ever wanted in life was her to cum in his mouth. He flicked and sucked at the her ultra sensitive clit and used two then three fingers to explore inside her wet core. Allison's skin vibrated with electricity. The follicles in her hair vibrated with pleasure. Her body clenched and released with every thrust of Bryson's fingers.

"I told you before, You are mine." A possessive fire roared through his body as he tasted every part of her.

Explosions fired off through Allison's body, over and over again. She reached down tangled her hands in his hair, moving with his mouth on her clit. He nipped her on her thigh with his teeth, and Allison almost fell off the table.

The contrast of immense pleasure and the interlude of pain bought Allison to the brink of ecstasy.

Without warning it started.

Overwhelming waves of electricity flowing through her body. Her body clenching and freezing up as he sucked the final resolve out of her. Allison collapsed on the table and signed, still convulsing from the intensity of her orgasm.

"I've never felt anything like that before." Before was good, but this was something all together different. It was surreal. Allison knew it wasn't only the act, it was who it was with. He grazed his hands against her arms and she bolted off the chair.

"Don't do that. I am way too sensitive for you to do that."

Bryson didn't let up. He stalked her around the kitchen, with Allison running around giggling like a school girl and Bryson following her. She stopped short, turned, grabbed Bryson and shoved him against the wall.

"Let's see if you can take what you give." She knelt down and unbuttoned his shorts. He looked down at her amused.

"Of course I can I--" Before he could get another word out, Allison grabbed his erection. She kissed the head and licked the drop of sweetness making an appearance.

"Shit," said Bryson.

Teasing him with her eyes, she looked up at Bryson while she guided him into her warm soft mouth. She caressed his erection with her tongue, feeling it harden as it pressed against her throat. He felt great in her mouth. The hardness with the ridges circling it, made ever time she took him in her mouth go straight to her core.

The more she got into it, the wetter she got. She worked him like she needed him in her mouth more than oxygen. She took her hand and massaged him while she sucked him, making sure her mouth offered enough slickness for her hands. She reached for his balls and took them into her mouth one by one, giving each of them her utmost attention, while her hands teased and softly pumped his erection.

Bryson's head fell back and he moaned his approval. He realized he was so hard it hurt. Looking at Allison handle him, claim him like she was with such power, made his knees weaken. He was glad he was being held up by the wall.

There eyes met while he was in her mouth, her tongue guiding and coaxing him to release. His breath caught unable to process all the small explosions occurring in his body at the same time. He was getting pleasure overload.

"You..my dear...knows how to please a --"

Not only was Allison handling him, claiming him and his body as hers, she looked damn sexy on her knees in front of him. Although she was on her knees, she held the upper hand.

She took him deeper and deeper down her throat while simultaneously massaging his balls. He couldn't take it anymore. He braced himself on the wall and emptied his orgasm into her mouth. She hesitated, taking it all in at first, so some of his thick juice fell down and around her cheek and mouth. But she didn't want the erotic moment to pass her by. She took it all flowing from him into her mouth, and swallowed.

She milked him until he had nothing left. She took it all.

Allison looked up at him with a naughty smirk on her face and licked her lips.

"How did you know how to do that. I mean, damn girl, what the hell was that?"

Allison was filled with such pride, it rivaled when she graduated magna cum laude from UGA.

"I guess I like you," and porn, lots and lots of porn, but she wasn't going to tell him that.

"I guess I like you too." He pulled her up from her position on the floor and hugged her. He then scooped her up and walked out of the kitchen. The sun was setting and the glass walls of the villa outlined a splash of oranges, yellows and reds across the once blue ocean.

"Where are you taking me?" asked Allison while wrapping her hands around his neck. Holding on, both physically and emotionally. She'd allowed herself in a moment of weakness to accept Bryson again not only in her bed, but in her heart.

Fear gripped her chest and momentarily made her unable to breath. She couldn't deal with him leaving and crushing her heart again. She wouldn't subject herself to that. Although he talked a good game, she didn't know if she could believe him.

"What's wrong?" He asked. He felt her stiffen up in his arms. "I'm not going to drop you."

"I know. Nothing is wrong. Where are we going?" But there was something wrong. How could she look at herself in the mirror after she just fell so easily after he dropped her like a hot potato.

"To my bedroom," he said. She half heard him. Instead she was beating herself up.

"We can't." He stopped.

"Why not?"

"I'm tired."

"I'll tuck you in."

"In my room." He looked at Allison unsure of her sudden withdrawal.

"In your room then."

He put her down as they reached her room. Although this was a new place for her, it felt comforting. She'd come to relax in the white and golden decorated room. She collapsed on the chair half staring, but not seeing anything in front of her. Instead her mind wondered what the heck she was doing. She didn't know and that scared her. She knew her and Bryson fit together sexually.

He drew out emotions in her she'd never imagined feeling, much less experiencing them over and over again. She liked his vibe when they were just hanging out, without the heaviness of their decisions.

He said he wanted to be with her. What did that mean? How? She'd just moved into her condo with Samantha. She had a life, she had plans. She was not going to give everything up to do what? Move in with Bryson.

He said he loved her, but it's not like he asked to marry her. She didn't want that anyway. Right?

A little frustrated at herself, she went to take a shower and slid into bed. She couldn't believe the night before she was sleeping on a beach scared, afraid and uncomfortable. Her head still buzzed at times but the aches in her body had all but subsided. She felt good overall.

So many things tried to get her attention. She worried if the baby she was carrying was still there after such trauma. There was no way for her to know. The little tyke was too small to move for her to feel, plus her mind told her nothing.

That made her so sad.

No, she didn't want to be pregnant, and she was going to give her baby up for adoption, but after the fear of dying and losing her little one, she changed her mind. Now, she couldn't think of anything else she wanted more.

Her parents.

Tears sprung to her eyes. In all the drama, she hadn't given much attention to her parents. They were one of the main reasons she was going to give her baby up for adoption. She planned to hide the pregnancy from them.

After all they were in NY. She figured she could hold them off for five or so months after she really started to show.

Who was she kidding, that was a terrible plan.

Good thing she decided to keep her baby.

*They would be so disappointed in me,* she thought. They'd given her everything she'd ever wanted. Her mother Celeste, even worked an additional ten years at the post office, put off retirement, so Allison wouldn't have college loans to contend with.

The tears started to pick up steam and she went into the bathroom for a tissue. They always wanted great things for her, and always supported Allison in anything she wanted.

When she'd told them she didn't want to become a lawyer but was majoring in accounting, they were disappointed, but they were happy as long as she was.

She knew she wouldn't be lucky this time.

Now, she would be an unwed single mother who got knocked up by a man she'd know all of a few hours.

Her mother would die.

She could see it now, her father would get this look on his face that screamed betrayal. She knew it. He would hate her for ruining the life he worked so hard for her to have, and he would be right. But as much as it would tear her heart out to tell them, she couldn't hide it any longer because it was no longer just about her. Hopefully the little tyke was still in there, and she would do everything in her power to keep her little one healthy.

*Now what about Bryson?*

# *SIXTEEN*

SHE WAS DOING IT AGAIN.

Running away. He'd told her he loved her and it didn't matter.

Never before had he told anyone he loved them except his family.

*This was unacceptable.*

He wouldn't allow her to keep running, as she had. But what could he do? He had to figure it out. He knew she wouldn't take his child away from him now that the cat was out of the bag. Everything was on the table. But he didn't have a plan.

He knew his parents were pulling out all the stops to find him. He gave them a few more days before they checked the Island. Although it was close, to where the plane went down, he didn't think they would have thought to check it already.

Good thing they could survive comfortably on the island for months. He knew it wouldn't take that long, and a rescue team would be here within the next few days. His mind ran on the sun splash resort takeover.

He almost wished he hadn't done the deal. He'd done it as a slight revenge against Deval.

He hated him.

He was a no good, spoiled corrupt little boy who was running his resort into the ground, which would affect Bryson's business. It's the rule of companions. There was an Anderson property right down the beach. If Deval drove sunsplash into the ground, it would reduce the value of Ander-Suns, his property as well, and reduce his business.

He'd seen it happen many times before. He despised when deals went bad because of third parties who had nothing to do with him, or his business. He wasn't going to sit and let that happen. The deal he offered Deval was a win win for both parties. He still wasn't trying to ruin the guy. He even gave him a nice severance package. That was a lot more than he would have gotten had the resort just imploded.

He hoped his parents would handle it. He did not want this to default back to Deval Patel. He knew the clause he signed, but who knew he'd be marooned on a island.

That problem was back on the main island.

Now he had to get his family back together. He knew the term "back together" was loosely drawn, but that was his goal. Get Allison to stop running, and trust him. To be a family. The thought of his child ran chills through his body.

He had enough to deal with. He wouldn't tackle dropping the news to his mother about Lauren and Allison just yet. He was no Mommas boy, but he still didn't want to disappoint his mother. She would probably think Allison got pregnant on purpose to get to the family money. That is something he would have to make sure didn't happen. All this thinking got him hungry and thirsty again.

He walked into the kitchen and saw Allison had the same idea. She was watching the darkness outside, eating a banana.

"Careful with that banana. If it's anything like me, It's going to explode all over you in a few seconds."

Allison nearly chocked. "You. Are. Crazy!"

"I thought you were tired?"

"I rested."

"How are you?" asked Bryson.

"Alright. I was just thinking."

"About?"

"Everything," said Allison.

"Me too."

"Really? What did you come up with?" asked Allison

"Absolutely nothing"

"Me too."

Bryson reached for some oranges and started cutting them to eat.

"Did you buy that condo?"

"Yes, me and Sam, we both went in on it. That way it was affordable."

"Do you like it?"

"I love it. We are just decorating now. We haven't decided on all the colors but it's coming along. Do you realize I don't know where you live."

"I spend most of my time in the Caymans but I've just taken a place in Atlanta."

"Where?"

"In Buckhead." Suspicious Allison asked, "Where in Buckhead?"

"Your building."

"Since when? I've never seen you there."

"I just decided on it after all your rave reviews."

"You aren't stalking me are you?"

"Sweetheart, we are marooned on a desert island. I don't have to stalk you."

Allison rolled her eyes. "So why are you moving into my building?"

"Because I'm not going to let you keep running and hiding from me."

"That sounds like stalking to me. "

"I'm not stalking you Allison. I can live where I want. I own the building, I can double live where I want. The worst case scenario is I'll be able to be with my kid."

"Worst case scenario?"

"Yes. You denying we are perfect for each other. I can't force you to do anything. The decision is up to you. Anyway, I'm going to bed, do you want to come?"

With the look that Allison gave him, he knew she'd gotten the wrong idea.

"To sleep. We could keep each other company."

That sounded great. Allison may not want to have sex with Bryson, she did, but felt it wasn't the best thing to do right now,  but his presence undeniably made her relax.

Plus the killer coconut and cream scent he was sporting didn't hurt. The idea of cuddling into his big hard body was very welcoming. She took his hand and she went to the simply decorated master bedroom to sleep.

And cuddle.

# *SEVENTEEN*

IN ALL THE YEARS Celeste imagined going to the beautiful Cayman Islands, it was never because her only daughter was missing in a plane crash. These things happen in movies, not in real life. She felt disconnected and everything felt unreal.

The fantasy fell flat even though they were chauffeured from NY in a private plane and ushered to an oversized mansion on the island. Thomas, her loving husband of twenty-four years sat beside her in the black lincoln town car. She stared at his strong masculine face and admired the knowledge and experience age had improved upon him.

His stoic demeanor only meant a storm was brewing underneath. He was doing everything he could to hold it together, everything to not break everything, or break down and cry with a broken heart.

Celeste knew Allison was his heart.

Without her, he would crumble up and die. If not physically, then mentally and emotionally.

Many of Celeste's friends didn't understand how she could nurture such a close relationship between father and daughter. Many of them confided in her that they would be jealous of how close Thomas and his daughter were, but not Celeste. She found it deeply rewarding and sweet. The fact that she could give her husband and daughter such a loving friend for each other meant the world to her. Now, they may all lose each other, and Celeste was shaking with fear.

Thomas sensed the increased tension in the car and moved closer to his wife. Without saying anything he pulled her into him and she nestled her head onto his shoulder. They'd been though much. You don't live over sixty years on earth without having your share of troubles. However, they always got through it because they had each other and nothing, no problem, could ever trump that.

Until now.

Thomas stroked Celeste's hair until he felt her calm slightly. She was his rock, as he was hers. They were both trying to hope for the best, but preparing for the worst and it was killing both of them, slowly.

Their Allison might be gone, and according to Thomas, someone was responsible for it, and he wouldn't sleep until he found out who it was.

The chauffeur opened the door and they got out of the limo. They were greeted by two expensively dressed people.

Thomas figured it was the boys parents. They were older, in their late sixties early seventies it seemed. Either they had the boy late, or the boy was a man.

"Bryson Anderson," said Bryson Sr. and reached for Thomas's hand to shake. "Sorry to be meeting under these circumstances, and this is my wife Antoinette."

Bryson Sr. held out a strong hand for Thomas who took it with an equal amount of strength attached to it. Each man knew the other was sizing them up. Neither was going to back down. Thomas shook Antoinette's dainty hands sensing a lot more strength than what was displayed to him.

"Mr. Anderson, I'm Thomas Caine and this is my wife Celeste. What do you know?" Bryson Sr appreciated a man who got down to business.

"Our investigators have not determined what happened to the plane," said Bryson Sr. as he turned and started on the path to the front door while everyone followed him. "They have nothing definitive, but suspect foul play."

That stopped Thomas up short. "Foul play? You mean this wasn't an accident?"

The thought that his daughter could be caught up in a death trap made him see red. His twenty years as a reporter working for the Daily News in New York had shown him countless victims through no fault of their own. He'd written about men and women being in the wrong place at the wrong time, and he refused to accept the same fate for his daughter.

Bryson Sr. knew this was going to be difficult. The love, fear and anger was rolling off Thomas and his wife in droves.

"That is what our investigators said. They are still working on it."

Bryson Sr. understood the anger, but he would only let it go so far. After all, his son was in this too. Antoinette looked on the verge of tears again, and he didn't want to do or say anything that would send her over the edge.

"Are there people after your son Mr. Anderson?"

It was a question Bryson Sr. tried not to consider, but faced with it, smacked dab in his face, his mind considered the unthinkable.

"I don't know who would be interested in harming my son. He's a good man who makes an effort to do the right thing. He's even decided to run for Public Office."

"Then is someone after you?"

"Of course not." Just like that Thomas had gone where no man should go, and question whether their actions could have led to their child getting hurt. The nerve of this stranger.

"Don't you dare ask me such questions. I will not have you walk into my home with such an accusatory stance. You can leave."

"I'm not leaving without my daughter. She went on a plane registered to the Anderson family and as far as I'm concerned, you are responsible for her."

Thomas's anger fought to hold on to someone or something to blame. Someone who would be accountable for him not having his daughter, someone who could bring her back. He had none of that, because he knew Bryson Sr. didn't have his daughter, or even knew where she was, or if she was alive.

But that mattered little.

"I will-"

"Where were they going?" Celeste's voice broke through the rancor which surprised everyone because everyone forgot she was still there.

"What?" asked Bryson Sr.

"Where were they headed?"

"They were headed to his private island. Forty five minutes after they took off, the pilot sent a distress signal and that was the last we heard of them."

"How far is the Island from here?" asked Thomas regaining his composure.

"About an hour," said Bryson Sr.

They'd reached the dining room now, and the table was set and waiting for them. Food was displayed in the middle of the massive dining room table but no one, from Bryson Sr, Antoinette, Celeste or Thomas was hungry.

"So, they were only fifteen minutes away,." said Thomas, hope blossoming in his voice.

"Yes about fifteen minutes." Was there an echo in here, questioned Thomas with his eyes but he didn't address the other man with his sarcasm. Everyone was on edge, no need to exasperate it.

"Has anyone checked the island?" asked Thomas. "They may have been able to make it there if it was only fifteen minutes away." It sounded unlikely even to his ears but it wasn't over until all avenues were checked.

"Mr. Caine, I know how hard this is for you but–"

"Don't but me Bryson. Obviously, no one has checked the island to see if any survivors made it there. Have you found any bodies?" It hurt so much for those words to leave Thomas's mouth, he thought he would black out.

"No, not yet, but there could be many different reasons for that," said Bryson Sr. He was trying to level out

Thomas's hope, not wanting the other man to wish too much for something that seemed unlikely at best.

"Never mind that, how soon can we get out there to check the island?"

"I'll have to check with my people and depending on the weather, tomorrow."

"How big is the island?" asked Thomas.

"About five square miles, " said Bryson Sr.

"Alright, But, I don't know if you want to fly out there, those kids are probably going to be scared out of their minds of flying right now," said Thomas with a smirk on his face.

Thomas hadn't smiled since he heard Allison was missing.

"Alright, You guys have had a long flight and probably want to get some sleep. I'll get everyone up to speed and they'll set off tomorrow," said Bryson Sr.

"They? I'm going with them."

"No you're not." Bryson Sr. didn't want any undue surprises on this rescue mission, and a civilian would only hurt the expedition. Plus, in case there was anything terrible that happened to both Bryson Jr. and Allison, he didn't want the parents to be the ones to see it first.

"Let the professionals do their jobs. There will be rescue personnel as well as medical personnel in case they are needed. I don't want anyone having to use man power to look after you."

He had a point.

"I'll see you tomorrow then. Where will the command center be?"

"In here. I can organize and monitor everything from here."

"Good Night." Everyone said goodnight, and the butler ushered the Caine's to their quarters.

Antoinette turned to her husband, joy and appreciation breaming from her. Thomas wasn't the only one he should have been worried about quelling hope of a fairy tale happy ending to this incident.

"Thank you so much." She reached for him and kissed him on the forehead.

"Anything for my family." She knew he meant it, but in the past, he'd done for many more people than his family, in many more personal ways. But she wasn't going to consider that now. Her husband was going to rescue her Bryson, and all of his previous transgressions meant nothing.

"I love you," whispered Antoinette as her mouth brushed his ear.

"I love you too." He meant every word with every fiber of his being. He loved this woman, with her golden eyes and caramel skin.

"I'm sending the calvary honey, they're going to get Bryson back for us." Bryson Sr. looked into his wife's trusting eyes and hoped he was telling the truth.

# *EIGHTEEN*

ALLISON WOKE UP TO a hard body elevated above her stroking her stomach. She looked up into the most handsome face she'd ever seen. A big smile laced with mischief greeted her. She'd never woken up with Bryson beside her before, and it felt great. The six hundred count sheets and the cool sweetness of his scent made her relax into him even more. She didn't want it to end.

"You snore," said Bryson.

"What?" He'd managed to push her out of the sweetness of her thoughts.

"I said you snore, sleepy head?"

"I do not. I sleep like a baby."

"Who snores. I figured I wouldn't disturb you, maybe it would alert the proper authorities to our location."

"Whatever," said Allison. He didn't see it but Allison gathered a thick fluffy pillow and belted Bryson with in on the side of his head. He fell sideways on the bed like he'd been hit with an anvil and reached for a pillow of his own to defend himself.

Allison got up to drop a fatal blow to the body when she was ambushed by two pillows coming at her. She retreated to the bed and feigned surrender.

"That's not fair you know."

"There are no rules in pillow fighting."

"Yeah well, it's still not fair."

"I could get use to this," said Bryson, stroking Allison's arm again as he took his place beside her and placed her hand on his arm.

"Me too," said Allison. Before she'd fallen asleep, she considered her options. She liked, maybe even loved Bryson., but she didn't know if what she was doing was the right thing. What would her mother say, or even her Father. OMG.

"What are you thinking?" Asked Bryson.

"What I'm going to tell my parents."

"Before you can do that, do you know what it is you are going to do?"

"About what?"

"About us obviously, or do you not see this breathtakingly gorgeous specimen of a man laying next to you."

Ignoring his comment, Allison sat up and took a serious look at the father of her baby. He was gorgeous. His dark hair, beautiful golden eyes and kissable lips were to die for.

"I want to give us a try." Sensing the seriousness of her words, Bryson sat up and faced her.

"What brought this about?"

Allison ran her fingers through her hair to buy her some time. She didn't have an exact answer to that. Was it his proclamation of love, how he'd taken care of her, how intensely in love she felt, or was it everything he did, how he tried to please her. She didn't know. Maybe it was the little Bryson growing inside of her.

"I don't know. We get along good, you're kind of fun and OK looking. So why not?"

"Ok looking? Do you need glasses?"

"Stop playing around and stop being so vain."

"I'm kidding of course. But you did forget you are carrying my child."

"Our child."

"Ah, no, my child. Wait and see, that kid is going to be a spitting image of me." The pride and joy coming from Bryson had Allison spinning. Her heart expanded with every word that he said. She instantly felt amazing and terrible at the same time. She'd held this from him and wasn't going to tell him. How could she have been so cruel. She was trying to hurt him, as he'd hurt her.

"I'm sorry for not telling you about the pregnancy."

"I'm sorry when you woke up that morning I wasn't there." Bryson took Allison's hands in his. "I hope we've cleared the air, because I want to show you something and I don't want to take you there mad."

"I wasn't mad by the way. I didn't trust you."

"I call it mad. What do you want to eat? I'm making breakfast."

"Whatever you have, you did a great job for dinner. Are you some type of trained chef?"

"No, I like to cook what I eat, so I was kind of forced to make sure it tasted good. I don't eat fast food so my choices are limited to what I cook for myself, mainly."

"No fast food? Come on, you don't know what you're missing."

"I do know what I'm missing that's why I don't touch it. Wait until I'm cooking for you everyday, you won't want anything to do with fast food."

"Bryson, be careful, you might spoil me and ruin it for the next guy."

Bryson stopped and Allison almost ran into him. He turned and held Allison in his arms.

"I have you now, and I promise to never let you go. You are mine for now til' always."

Allison's knees buckled. See, he always did that. All she'd said was "try." It seemed like Bryson heard what he wanted. He sure felt good, and she slowly and completely fell into him, and submitted to his claim. When their lips touched, it felt like lightening erupting between them zapping their lips and hearts together. Bryson put his love and heat for her into the kiss. Allison received it with love and longing. She felt his erection against her as he kissed her greedily, taking her all in. She wanted to stay and satisfy her hunger for him, but she was actually hungry for food and that won over her other hunger. Reluctantly she broke the kiss and looked at him. She hoped she was hungry from a little baby still growing inside her.

"Let's finish this later, right now, I am very hungry."

With a deep smoky laugh, Bryson kissed her on the forehead and started towards the kitchen again.

"How about some scrambled eggs fbrentine with asiago and Romano cheese, toast and hash browns?"

"Wow, that seems complicated. Can I help?"

"Yes, you can keep me company and enjoy all that I have to give."

Allison smiled and counted her lucky stars. She would never imagine such happiness. She hoped it would never end.

There weren't many things that got Deval Patrick out of bed before three P.M in the afternoon, but today he was getting his resort back. The dark designer sunglasses guarded his bloodshot eyes from the unforgiving sun. Twenty minutes tops and all of the stress and worry that was plaguing him for weeks would be lifted. Once he had Sun-splash resort back under his ownership, he was going to do some house cleaning. Firing people he came to realize did not have his best interest at heart.

Like Marjorie, the one who alerted Bryson Jr. to the inner workings of the resort. He wondered what was going to be in it for her. It didn't matter now. He inhaled the end of his cigarette, threw it on the ground and stepped on it. He could have used the cigarette disposal atop the garbage can instead, but Deval never took the time to look around or consider before making a move. He entered the building. The cold air made him alert. Ready.

A few days ago this meetings meant complete and utter failure. He was going to be signing away his company to Anderson Properties, AKA Bryson Anderson Jr.

*That bastard* thought Deval. Yes, Deval had squandered the money left to him by his hard working immigrant parents. Yes, he'd run the Sun-splash resort almost into the ground with his mismanagement of funds and people. Yes, he was a terrible business man who'd mortgaged and gambled everything he had plus, he owed the Mariachi Family money.

A lot of money. But that was all behind him now. Before the ink dried on the contracts, he would be alright. He would pay Anthony Mariachi the installment payments they'd agreed on and get on with his life. Today, with Bryson Jr. out of the picture, he felt he'd gained a new life.

Walking into the conference room with it's twice shined marble floors, rich mahogany furniture and tall soft leather chairs, Deval felt out of place.

This wasn't his so called scene. In the arms of exotic women around the world, in an alcoholic induced semi coma, that was his scene. He couldn't wait to get back into one of those embraces.

He wasn't the first one in the room. Everyone looked up at him as he entered. Two white haired men with eyes that saw more than they needed, looked up from their calculators, and the mounds of paperwork in front of them.

*They must be the accountants,* thought Deval. He walked over to Scott Wench and shook his hand.

"Scott."

His lawyer looked at Deval and they walked together to the table.

"Are we ready.

"We are waiting for Mr. Stevenson to join us."

"Mr. Wha--?"Sweat started to pool on Deval's eyebrows.

"His brother-in-law Nicolas is taking his place."

"No one told me this. I thought this was going to be part of the default clause and I would get to leave here without selling the resort."

"Look, I know what you are saying. I'm having one of my guys fine comb the contract to see if we can have the entire deal default on account that Bryson Jr. isn't here. I don't remember if we specified that or not."

Anger, fear and panic began to well up deep within Deval. He tried to push it back but it attacked him, flowed through him like the blood in his veins. He took off his dark expensive sun glasses and wiped the sweat forming on his nose. This was unacceptable.

If he wasn't there to sign the papers, what was he still doing there. Suddenly, he picked up one of the leather chairs and hefted it across the room.

"I made a deal with Bryson Jr. and if he won't stand up to it by being here, then neither do I."

The men in the room, with their dark gray suits on didn't breathe for what seemed like years. They didn't know what to do. They were only there to do their jobs, not to be apart of a crazy person's vendetta. One gray suit looked for a way out the room, but saw Deval was in front of the only exit. Gray suit number two reached for his bag as if something in there could save him from what ever was coming next.

Deval steamed towards the door. Before he reached it, Nicolas Stevenson stepped into the room with his lawyer in tow. They would have bumped into each other if it wasn't for Deval turning to his left at the last minute.

Nicolas wasn't as handsome as Bryson Jr., but they had a similar build. Built tall and strong like a linebacker, Nicolas filled his expertly tailored suite to perfection.

"Where are you off to Mr. Patel." He checked his watch then said, "We are right on time."

"I am leaving Nick, I was expecting Bryson. Seeing as though he's not here, I have no further business here."

Deval tried to push past Nick but got nowhere.

"That's Mr. Anderson to you. My brother was involved in an accident and that's the only reason he's unable to be here. I am here as his representative. We are ready and able to close this deal today. I don't see what difference it makes that Bryson isn't here."

"Because he signed the contract."

"This wasn't a personal sale. This was a business to business contract and I am a Representative of Anderson Properties."

"The last time I checked you weren't part of Bryson's company in any official capacity. This sale is unacceptable, you cannot sign on either the company's behalf or Bryson, so If you would excuse me."

Deval knew what he was doing. Knew how Nick was excluded from his wife's family's business. Everyone knew. Catch him at a hotel bar or a pub after three drinks and he would tell anyone close to him about the unfairness of his exclusion. It was definitely a sore spot. Now it seemed Nick was trying to take Bryson's place. The flash of anger and the narrowing of Nick's eyes as he looked at Deval happened so fast, most people in the room missed it except Deval. A small smirk grew on his face. He'd won.

"The last time you checked must have been before today because I am now apart of Anderson Properties."

A smug smile creep-ed onto Nick's face. Checkmate you smug bastard.

The two men faced off together in the conference room. Searching for time, Deval looked to his lawyer. Scott gave him nothing. Shaking his head he turned to Nick.

"My lawyer and I need time to verify if what you are saying is accurate. We will check with the proper parties to make sure you are eligible to sub in for Bryson."

"That works. Let's meet back here on Friday. Just make sure the default clause is out. You are the one who needs more time, not me."

"Fine, but I can't do Friday. Monday at three works better for me. But no more sub in's. It's either you, Bryson or the deal is off," said Deval as he finally made his way past Nick. Now that Bryson wasn't running for office, his contacts may not be interested in Deval's problems enough to help him out. He needed a solution and fast.

Allison was full after breakfast. Full of love, desire and food. All she wanted to do was lay around the house and figure out a way to get word back, especially to her parents that they were OK, more than OK if you asked her.

If she only knew Morse Code. But Bryson had assured her his parents would send someone looking here soon and they shouldn't worry too much. He wouldn't let her lay around and sulk.

"Come on let's go." Bryson appeared in front of her as she lounged on the softest leather couches she'd ever felt. Allison was enjoying snuggling into the soft fabric as it wrapped around her body.

"No. I don't want to go anywhere. Plus look around, there's no where to go."

"There are plenty of places to go." Bryson took up a soft pillow and lobbed it at Allison. She moved slightly to the left to avoid the offending pillow and started to giggle.

"Get up, come on let's go." Allison didn't move but stayed on the couch giggling. "Am I going to have to pick you up and take you there?"

"You wouldn't."

"Oh yes I would." Before the last word left his lips, Bryson moved towards the couch slowly with Allison in his sights. She scooted from side to side out of his reach when he got close enough to catch her. Surrendering, she let herself be captured. He gently lifted her in his arms, and she wrapped her hands around his neck and inhaled his sweet sent.

"Where are we going?" asked Allison

"You'll see."

"I don't like surprises," said Allison

"Too Late."

Bryson pushed the back door of the villa open and walked onto the back tiled patio while Allison used her hand to guard her eyes from the sun. Bryson continued to carry Allison as he left the patio and continue onto the beach.

He reached the shores of the ocean and put Allison down. The pink sundress she had on flowed in the wind as she took in the vastness of the ocean.

"It's beautiful isn't is?" asked Bryson.

"Yes. It's beautiful, but overwhelming at the same time."

Allison looked right and left. She saw sand and blue ocean as far as the eye could see. The waves crashed onto the shore with a calming rhythm, softly hiding the power the ocean held. The vastness of the landscape, the never ending scene of the ocean and sand made Allison feel small and insignificant.

"I feel so small compared to all this," said Allison as her arms tried to take it all in.

"Well, we are."

"Doesn't that scare you."

"No. Why should it?" Bryson wrapped his hands around Allison's neck and together they rocked back and forth to the sound and rhythm of the waves.

"Because we are so small and helpless in the face of nature."

"We've survived this long, so maybe we shouldn't fear it as much as we should respect it."

"You say respect, I say fear."

"What are you so afraid of?"

"Dying." Disappointing my parents, losing my baby etc etc, but she didn't voice those fears.

"You're not going to die. You're young. What are you like thirty, thirty two?"

With an incredulous look on her face Allison smacked him on the arm.

"I'm twenty four smart ass."

"Even more reason. What are you some kind of hypochondriac?"

"Look, I hate when old people tell young people it is impossible for them to die or something because they think you people will live forever."

To Bryson, those were fighting words. He took his hands from around Allison and turned to face her. Allison knew she'd hit the nerve she was going for.

"So you think I'm old do you?"

"Did I say you were old? Dear me. How rude?" Allison put her right hand to her chest in mock embarrassment.

"Well this old man knows how to make you cum pretty well doesn't he."

"What a way to toot your own horn."

"If my woman won't do it, then I have to do it myself."

His woman. Allison turned those words around in her head. It had a nice ring to it, but she wasn't going to let him off that easily.

"Your woman? the last time I checked I was no one's woman."

"Check again. The moment I set eyes on you, you became my woman. You just didn't know it yet."

"Plus I'm still a girl."

"Bryson let out a hefty laugh.

"Alright, you are my girl. I love you, my girl Allison."

He turned Allison to face him and looked into her dark eyes. Eyes that swallowed him up with their depths. The quiet of the crashing waves and vastness of the ocean around them made the two small insignificant beings meld closer together as one. There lips touched. Birds began to sing and everything became more vivid, more colorful. The air felt alive. Bryson swiped his tongue between Allison's lips,requesting entrance to her.

She wondered if he was trying to gain entrance to her soul.

She let him in. Slowly at first, then she started kissing him intensely. Her body was filled with liquid fire running from between her legs throughout her body. She loved Bryson. However they had gotten together, she loved him and she knew it. She broke their contact and starred into his golden eyes.

"I love you Bryson." Tears threatened to spring from her eyes. "I don't know why I'm like this now, but I'm overwhelmed by the ocean, what's happened and how I feel about you."

Bryson reached for her and held her close to his heart.

"I love you Allison, more than I've ever loved anyone ever."

They stayed that way for what seemed like an eternity.

Bryson tall and towering over Allison rocked back and forth in front of the crashing Caribbean waves.

"Can you swim?" asked Bryson.

"Yes."

"This is what I brought you out here for, let's go swimming."

"I don't have a bathin-. Oh it's still light outside."

"Barely." The rich orange, reds and blues of sunset was washing over the sky. Allison realized she'd just had breakfast.

"Plus there's no one else here. We are on a deserted island remember." As she protested, Bryson took off his shirt to reveal a broad muscular body with ripples of muscles etching his back. The gorgeous glint in his eye never left Allison as he slipped out of his shorts. There he was staring at Allison in all his gloriousness.

His naked body was a feast for her eyes. Wide muscular shoulders tapering at the waist and leading to a slowly rising arousal between his legs. Allison took in the face, and butterflies started waking up in her stomach. Bryson reached out his hand.

"Come with me for a swim. The water is right."

After hesitating for a few more seconds, Allison slipped out of her pink sundress and joined, her naked body with her naked man in the ocean.

The water was cold until Allison dunked her head underwater. It now felt perfect. The sand under her toes and the soft current of the waves wrapping around her body brought a smile to her face. She was still weary of the ocean but it felt freeing. They swam together a little, enjoying the water and each other. Playfully touching each other until the moon shone bright in the sky.

The full moon brought as much light as street lamps would. They staggered out of the water and collapsed onto the sand. The tide washed under them as they stared up at the stars. Allison reached over and swung her left leg over Bryson while resting her head on her hand.

"So Bry"

"Don't call me Bry." Allison played with his chest and let her fingers wonder down to his stomach and back again. Slowly she teased him with her fingers.

"Why not, I like it."

"I don't. I like Bryson."

"Or Daniel."

"Or Daniel." Allison stopped petting him and just stared, scorn starting to develop in her eyes.

"None of that." Bryson rolled on top of Allison, balancing himself on his elbows.

"No getting back into upset Alli mode."

He started to place butterfly kisses along Allison's set jaw. She was getting upset.

"I'm just saying. If you didn't have anything to hide why did you give me a fake name."

He placed more kisses on her chin, moving his way to her neck. With every kiss her anger dissipated, but only slightly.

"I did have something to hide. I didn't want you to know my families name. I like to be anonymous."

More kisses, headed towards her neck. He knew the spot behind her ears would drive her insane and with the slow direction he was headed, they both knew what would happen.

"You did say you owned the building."

"I knew you wouldn't believe me."

"So why say it?"

"For moments like this and I could say I was being totally truthful Plus, it's fun."

One of Bryson's hands started to caress her thigh moving slowly but deliberately up her body.

"But you weren't, your name isn't Daniel." Daniel came out as a sigh. Bryson graduated from butterfly kisses to having his tongue play hickey with her neck. Stopping only long enough to say, "My middle name is Daniel. So not technically a lie."

Bryson continued making love to Allison's neck with his tongue. Her tits weren't getting any love so, he moved lower. Sucking in a breath while wrapping her legs around his hard body, the last of Allison's anger left.

*Middle name, yeah, that explains it,* she thought.

She opened her eyes and stared at the black sky with its bright stars. The light of the moon made Bryson look like he was shinning and wrapped in silver. Her head went back into the sand as he nipped at her nipple.

"Damn," were the only words her brain could put together. She closed her eyes and opened her body to the night. She felt the openness of the beach. She felt it stretching for miles around. The ocean washed up around her cooling her down as Bryson heated her up.

He looked at her lovestruck, her dark eyes shinning in the moon light and captured her lips with his. Their lips danced together under the moon light with the ocean lapping up around them.

Allison wanted more.

She wanted him, hot and hard inside of her. Filling her with everything he had to offer. Stroking her inside and out, physically and mentally. She raised her hips to signal what she wanted.

KayAnna Kirby

"Tuh tuh tuh eager beaver," said Bryson while rubbing his hips between Alli's legs.

"I like teasing you." Allison felt his hardness. It must take a considerable amount of will not to do what she asked him for.

But she'd had enough. Caught off guard, she was able to roll Bryson onto his back and straddle him and hold his hands above his head on the sand. Surprise will usually win out over strength. He semi tried to roll her back but Alli held her ground.

"You are at my mercy now." A sheepish grin made it's way across Bryson's face until Allison went to his nipple and nipped it. All laughing and kidding washed away with the tide.

Allison teased and nipped him, on his ear, his chin, his chest and nipples. She moved her hips around on him, making sure to tease the head of his erection with her hot wet middle. His breath was uneven and she knew she didn't have long before he overpowered her, having his way with her in the process She almost wanted that, but she was in control now. Just when she knew he'd had enough teasing, she reached between her legs and slowly slid his hardness inside her.

His hard erection meeting with her hot wet core caused an explosion for both of them. He sprang up to sitting position, as Allison made herself comfortable. She kissed him hard them. She couldn't get enough of his taste. His cool coconut scent engulfing his entire body. He hadn't shaved and the rough stubble on his face felt great.

She started moving her hips taking every inch of him. His hands grabbed her ass and tried to guide it his way.

"This is my show," said Allison.

She refused his dominance and rode him to the rhythm of the waves. Liquid fire spread through her from her fingers to her toes. He pulled her hair back to expose her throat and moved his hips with hers as he ravaged her neck. When their bodies melded as close as they could get, Allison let out a loud erotic moan. She felt like she was flying, free with his erection teasing her to release her liquid heat.

Every thrust, every meeting of their hips drew Alli closer to the end. Her release was building, gathering energy and life stretching up her stomach, to her nipples and gathering in her veins. She tried to hold it back.

She tried to process the unbelievable pleasure mixed with the pain of holding back her release and she still didn't want it to end. She rode slower, but Bryson would have none of it. He thrust into her hard and strong, breaking down the walls she'd erected to hold on longer. Brick by brick she built up resistance. Brick by brick, thrust by thrust Bryson knocked it down until she reached the point of climax.

She tensed, UN-breathing, every muscle in her body straining against the assault of ecstasy flowing through her trying to get out. Bryson nipped her nipple and Allison lost it, she collapsed on his chest as sweet liquid flowed onto his erection.

But he wasn't done yet. Everything was ultra sensitive for Allison. He lifted her off him and she knelt on the soft wet sand. Wind blew her hair around her face and the ocean crashed louder around her. The music of the water and sound of the wind made a small wicked smile cross her lips.

*Holy shit*, she thought *I'm having sex on a beach*.

It was so...naughty and she loved it. The fresh smell of the sea felt too free and open to have sex. She felt like people were watching her make love, seeing her face as she took Bryson into her.

Everything felt open. She took a deep breath and the rush of the earth invaded her body. Fresh, clean, open and utterly naughty.

Bryson used his fingers to play with Allison's opening, teasing her entrance with his fingers. The sensation shot right through her causing her head to go back and her back to arch. He'd gotten her right where he wanted her. Using his hardness to tease her, putting it in a little way and taking it out, running it around her core and taking it out drove Alli crazy.

"Stop teasing me--"

She looked back at him and saw a wicked, mischievous smile gracing his lips. His dark hair shown silver in the moon light; looking sexy as hell didn't excuse the torture he was doing to her. At the last minute she pushed back and surprised him by taking him all in at once.

All teasing stopped. Bryson palmed her round ample ass as he pumped into her. Slowly at first, touching every inch, her softness engulfing him, welcoming him, teasing him, driving him crazy. They fit together unquestionable. Then more urgent. Harder stronger strokes. His hard body was getting harder by the second.

Getting into a rhythm with the ocean water washing up on his knees and the wet sand offering a great foundation for his knees he started to slap her ass. Allison moaned, pleasantly surprised by the erotic pleasure she got from it. A lot of pleasure with a little pain. Her brain started to fuzz. She was going to cum again. Before she did, she was going to show him what she was working with.

She opened her legs a little wider and started moving her hips around against Bryson. He couldn't take it any longer. His body tensed for a second before releasing everything into Allison. She was already pregnant, couldn't do any harm now.

They both rolled onto the sand and looked at the stars. The sky was peaceful, their bodies were peaceful, their minds at ease. The temperature was still warm, although the sun went down hours before. Bryson picked her up, and carried her into the ocean. They kissed and stroked and fondled until the wee hours of the morning. Soking and feeding the fire of each other a few more times before sunrise.

They hardly made it back to the house before the sun rose. They stumbled onto the sand spent from pleasing each other throughout the entire night.

This was the happiest Bryson had ever been. He carried Alli over the threshold and deposited her wet body into the shower. He watched her soap up through the glass shower doors with the goofiest smile he'd ever made. He could watch her forever, and if no one came to rescue them, it would be alright with him.

# *NINETEEN*

*MAYBE HE DIDN'T HAVE to "get rid" of Nick,* thought Sean. It was messy and too much work.

*My goodness, who would have thought this would have been so hard.*

Bryson was already out of the picture, getting rid of his brother in law would only bring undue attention to the situation. For the last few hours he'd gotten more sober than he'd wanted to be. He lit a cigarette and inhaled the strong stringent smoke into his lungs. He exhaled, making circles with the smoke without focusing on the tourists walking around. The espresso on the tile table in front of him was getting cold so he finished it with a swig. This was a bustling part of town, down by the docks; everyone watching the cruise ships go by. The warm sun warmed his skin as he tried to figure out his next step. Selling wasn't an option. He wondered if anyone else knew of the payoff Bryson had put into the deal. His cell phone startled him out of his thoughts.

"Sean."

Yeah?"

"Just as a heads up, they are going to look for Bryson on his private island in the morning."

"Why? That seems like a waste of ti--"

"Look, I don't know or care about the whys of it. We both need him gone and there is a chance you didn't complete the job the first time."

"Things have changed, I want Bryson gone, but Nick is trying to take his place. What am I going to do about that?"

"Nick is not my problem-"

"I will be your problem if my resort is taken from me," said Sean.

"It's not being taken from you, it's being bought."

"Listen, I don't need an economics lesson here. Just take of Nick and I'll finish what I started if necessary," said Sean. He continued, "by the way, where did you get this intel from." Sean smiled to himself. He felt like a bona fide spy.

Intel.

He smiled again.

"From Nick. He thinks I'm his friend. He want's to be apart of the family business so much, he whine's to whoever will listen. Sean considered what his confidante was telling him

"Anything else?"

"Yeah, there may be a girl with him."

They slept the day away. When Bryson opened his eyes, the sun was almost all the way to the West. He looked and saw Alli asleep snoring away, her dark thick hair spread over the white pillows. She looked comfortable, restful, peaceful. His chest swelled with the realization that he was partly responsible for her current state. His pride was overwhelming. He got up and went to the kitchen to make coffee.

When they got back to civilization, they were really going to have to return to a normal schedule. He choose the Jamaican Blue Mountain Coffee beans from the cupboard and placed it into the coffee grinder. It smelled great. The  aromas invading his senses made him speed up the process.

As he ground the beans, he didn't hear the plane land a few hundred feed from the beach. He didn't look out the expansive bay windows as he poured two cups of hot liquid into two coffee mugs. If he had, he would have seen a lone body traveling up to the beach on a silent raft dressed in all black. He placed the coffee on a try and carried it to the bedroom. He hated when anyone woke him up and was concerned Allison was the same way. The coffee would be a form of peace offering. He reached the master bedroom and he could see she was stirring.

"Morning beautiful."

A lazy smile glistened on her face. Her dimple and wild hair making her look innocent. "Morning? Already?"

Bryson walked over to the side table and placed the tray beside the bed.

"It's really late afternoon. I brought you coffee."

Bryson handed Alli a large cup of hot steaming coffee. She took it graciously wrapping her fingers around the cup and letting the warmth travel through her body. Bryson placed the cup to his mouth, but movement outside the window caught the corner of his eye.

He felt a sense of relief and extreme sadness. The rescue team was here and his time alone with Allison was coming to an end. Just as well, he had tons of things to take care of on the mainland, like making Allison his wife. He was already thinking about how he was going to do it. He figured he would travel to New York and pick up a diamond from Tiffany's and go from there. He wanted to make it special, but hadn't figured out how to yet.

"I think our calvary is here."

Allison looked towards the window with the same sentiment Bryson had a minute ago. A look of relief and disappointment washed over her. She looked like she didn't know whether to jump up and down, or cry. She did neither. She sat there and stared out the window straining to see what Bryson had seen.

"I don't see anything."

Bryson looked out the window again, but didn't see anything either.

"Stay here, I'll be right back."

Bryson reluctantly pulled himself off the bed, put on his terry cloth white robe and went to the door that led outside. He was on the beach in a matter of seconds looking for the figure he saw.

A razor sharp jolt traveled through his body, his ears started buzzing and his blood pressure started to rise.

Something was wrong.

His senses were on high alert telling him to run, to take cover, but he didn't see anything, he didn't see any danger.

His skin felt prickly as he took slow methodical steps towards the side of the villa. Alert but telling himself to calm down, he made his way around the house. The sand masked the sound of his steps while he took quiet slow breaths. Something was not right and he was going to figure it out.

His future wife and child were in that house and he wouldn't let anything happen to them. His fingers flexed as he defensively trekked around the house. He made it around back and saw the jungle brush of the island looking ominous. All the other times he'd seen it, the brush was welcoming, promising adventure and fun.

Now it looked threatening and mysterious. He looked around seeing nothing, started talking himself into a calm he didn't have. He turned his back and started making his way to the villa. Allison was at the window, another one of Bryson's Terry Cloth robes hugging her body grasping her coffee cup in her hands. A wide smile graced her face.

She waved her hand above her head, saying hi, although he wasn't gone for more than two minutes. He watched her as he walked, more in love with her now than he was yesterday. Her deep dark eyes more trusting that it was almost a week ago. Allison's hand stopped waving but still hung in the air. One hand gripping her cup.

Her face became frozen, caught between words and a scream. Confused, he sped up. His blood pressure spiking making his heart knock against his chest. The buzzing started again in his ear and he wouldn't have been able to hear her if she was standing right in front of him.

His legs wouldn't move fast enough.

He had a primal urge to get to and protect his mate. Her arms were flailing now, coffee cup no where to be seen. His legs dug into the sand struggling against gravity to move.

That's when he felt it.

A searing cutting pain, shooting from his shoulder blade. Something tore through him, causing his body to jerk forward and fall face first onto the sand.

His brain wouldn't process what happened. His primal need to protect Allison gave him strength to get up on his hands and knees. As long as he was moving closer to her, to his family, it would be alright. A loud boom sounded to the left of him and another searing pain tore through the back of his leg this time. He collapsed on the sand once again, strength and energy flowing out of him like the thick red liquid coloring the sand.

He heard it then, Allison's scream; shrill, loud, scared. He tried to move, but couldn't. The darkness was threatening to take over and he wouldn't let that happen.

Couldn't. But...


Allison ran though the house stunned and shaking. She'd just witnessed Bryson, her dear Bryson shot twice by the same person who was chasing her. She ducked into a bedroom and slipped under the bed. Shaking, body numb and tears streaming down her eyes, Allison tried to not breath, not to make a sound. Her heart sounded too loud to her ears and she willed it to quiet down.

Someone wanted to kill her?

That made her breath catch.

Kill her? What did that mean? Kill her. She curled up into a ball and started to hum in her mind. Literally her life flashed before her eyes...again.

Friends, family, schools, jobs. She hadn't done anything. She would leave the world with nothing to show for it, taking her son or daughter with her. She felt like an insignificant gnat that was about to be snuffed out. She couldn't contain herself.

The shaking became overwhelming. She had to bite her lips to stop her teeth from shattering.

Fear gripped her soul.

Her mind trembled thinking about what would happen next. She was only twenty four she thought. Only twenty four.

The door creaked open and a black foot peeped in. Drums started beating in Allison's ears. She didn't want to die. She was starting to freak out. She couldn't believe this was how it was going to end.

She survived a plane crash and was going to be murdered in cold blood. Her parents, her friends, would hurt so bad.

She feared the pain. Would he shoot her, like he did Bryson.

Bryson.

She couldn't believe it. Everything was happening so fast. She found her love and now she would die. She wished she could just pass out until the whole thing was over. But the adrenaline pumping through her veins wouldn't allow her to.

He went to the closet and peered in, found nothing and turned to leave. Harsh curses left his mouth. Allison couldn't see his face. She closed her eyes readying herself for the inevitable.

Would she cry or beg? Those never worked. He kicked the wall and Allison almost screamed. He then turned and left the room.

It felt like hours as Allison laid in a fetal position under the bed.

It was only forty five seconds.

She regained her wits and realized that this may not be the end of her. With every passing second, Allison started to regain herself again along with a curious emotion, anger. This man had hurt her love, the father of her kid, threatened not only her but her baby. He'd attempted to kill off her family.

She wouldn't bring herself to think that Bryson was anything more than hurt. It was too much for her psyche to accept or consider. More seconds passed and she realized no one was going to come and save them. They were on their own.

Bryson was shot and bleeding on the sand. The longer he stayed out in the hot caribbean sun, soaking the sand with his blood, the harder it would be for him to wake up.

That was unacceptable.

She had no choice, for her family, Allison was going to risk it all.

Reaching out with her senses she listened. He was in the bedroom next to the kitchen. He was looking in every room. This man didn't seem too smart. Who wouldn't look under the bed for a potentially hiding person?

Alli didn't question her good fortune. She slid from under the bed, making sure she didn't breathe too loudly. The cold tile floor was a shock to her sweating soles but made her more alert. Alli slid against the wall and ran tip toeing on the tile to the kitchen. The tile floor masked any sound her bare feet might have made.

She reached the kitchen and momentarily panicked. The darkness of fear tried to push through her resolve. She froze, unable to move or think what she should do next.

Her head turned to the window and she saw her Bryson, passed out on the sand, wet red sand all around him. Tears sprung to her eyes, the burn of the onset of tears causing her to jump into action. She bent low and slowly went to the draw with the butcher knives.

Allison attempted to pull out the draw so slowly she felt it would take years to get her weapon. What was she going to do with it anyway?

He had a gun.

A creak in the draw made Allison abandon the butcher knife idea and hold her chest when her heart threatened to jump out of her chest.

He was getting closer. He would be in the kitchen in a matter of seconds. Frantic, Allison looked around, fear squeezing her heart. She was out in the open, if he didn't see her right away, he would see her as soon as he walked around the island in the kitchen.

A handle drew her attention and she quietly opened it. Inside she was rewarded with a heavy cast iron wok. She lifted it out of the cabinet without thinking and readied herself, crouched on the floor with her wok.

She didn't know if a cast iron wok would stop bullets, but she crouched and waited anyway. Forever and a day passed before she heard the man in the kitchen, cursing and going to the refrigerator for what seemed like a cold drink.

Allison watched his careless shadow. He was unaware he was the one being stalked. A high buzz started in Allison's ear. She was ready.

It was him or her. She knew she only had one chance to get this right. If she missed, her entire family would be gone.

He came over and placed his drink on the island, oblivious to the threat that existed below him.

Without thinking Allison rose slowly, like a snake biding her time before she pounced. The second after he saw her shadow behind him, he felt a hot breath on his neck, Allison swung the wok as hard as she could towards the back of his head, screaming from the dept of herself.

His head was no competition for the cast iron wok and the man collapsed to the floor. His gun flying across the marble floors to stop against the refrigerator.

Blood seeped from where the wok connected with the mans head but it wasn't enough. She didn't want him waking up and trying to kill her or her family again. She raised the wok over her head, and sent it down on his head again. His body jerked, but she saw that he was still breathing. His chest rose and fell slightly every few seconds. Allison searched the cupboards and used a large garbage bag to tie his hands and feet together the best she could. She ran into the pantry and got the broom and dustpan.

The gun looked ominous. She hated guns, was scared of them, but was more scared of him waking up and somehow getting the gun. If that happened, she was sure he wouldn't miss. She used the broom to sweep the gun onto the dustpan. With her arms stretched out in front of her, she carried it to the master bedroom and placed the entire dustpan in a draw. She ran back to the kitchen to make sure he was still there.

He was out like a light.

She wet some towels and dashed to the back door along with a jug of water. Allison felt like she was running in concrete. Her legs felt heavy and wouldn't move as fast as she wanted them to. Her heart pounded against her chest while sand wrapped around her toes.

Reaching Bryson, she poured the water onto where the blood was leaking from his body. He was hot, his skin burning to the touch. Maybe it was the sun beating down on him, but she feared he was getting feverish.

Bryson's chest still moved up and down. Blood was coming from his upper right shoulder, and his lower left leg. She used the water to wash the blood away, and almost fainted when she saw the two holes in his body.

She was running on adrenaline. No thought that came to her was considered. She only responded, acted, performed. She was being guided by instinct, by love.

She used the towels to wrap around his wounds trying to stop the free flow of blood. She placed his head in her lap and poured water over his face. His lips were chapped but she was out of water. She needed to leave him and go in the house for more water, but her heart resisted the move.

His head felt right in her lap as she stroked his hair. Scared if she left him, something would happen to him she stayed longer than she needed to. Finally she gently placed his head on the sand and ran to the house to fill up the jug with more water. She entered the house cautiously.

There was a killer in the kitchen.

He was still sprawled on the floor. She went to the sink and filled up her jug with water and ran it out to Bryson. When she placed his head back on her lap, he stirred. Hope soared in Allison.

"Come sweetie, it's me Alli,..."

He moaned.

"Here drink. She placed the jug to his lips and he weakly drank what he could from it. They stayed that way for hours until the orange, reds and blue of sunset started appearing.

Allison, face dried with tears was still stroking her Bryson. She had changed the towels on his wounds twice already and was getting worried he was losing too much blood. Hope was fading faster than the sun.

At least her family would be together. She broke down multiple times. She lamented on how short her time with Bryson had been. She tried her best, and her best wasn't good enough. She fought, she tried, but Bryson's life was slipping away, draining out of him. As she waited she looked at him and stroked his cheek and told him stories .

Stories about growing up in New York. Stories about her and Samantha playing hookie on half school days. She even told him they weren't exactly the coolest kids in school, and neither of them were ever invited to the hookie parties, so they usually went to bookstores and browsed.

A sad smile moved her lips as she told her stories. Stories she didn't know if he heard. She existed between anger, sadness, and nostalgia. She threw sand and whatever rocks she could find around, angry at her fate, and questioned what she did to deserve it. She wanted more. More time, more love, more everything.

Here she was on the verge of having nothing.

Then she heard it.

The sound of a helicopter landing on the other side of the house.

It sounded like hope.

# *TWENTY*

FEET TRAMPLED THROUGH THE house until they saw the figures sitting on the ground in the back. It was dark by now, so flashlights found the figures first. Men in all black clothing and the medical staff in all white surrounded Allison and Bryson. They were asking her questions but all she saw were their mouths moving.

She felt so tired. One of the people in white started again.

"What's your name?"

"Allison," she replied her mouth and throat dry.

"What happened?"

"That man shot my Bryson in the back."

Saying the words out loud started a new crying session. One of the medical men came around and guided her up but she wouldn't leave Bryson. Other medical staff worked on him and lifted him onto a stretcher. She walked beside Bryson, holding his hands as they guided him into the helicopter. They didn't walk through the house, but around it.

There was only one helicopter on the beach. But she saw a small plane a few hundred feet out into the ocean and a inflatable yellow boat, washed up on shore. That must have been how that man sneaked up on them, thought Allison.

"The man who did this is in the kitchen." They already knew and she looked and saw medical staff tending to him in the kitchen.

Where were they going to put him. There was only one helicopter

She settled inside the cramped helicopter, and held Bryson's hand while wrapping her fingers around his. Her head fell back against the window, and she breathed the breath she didn't know she was holding. She watched as the medics started an IV for Bryson and gave him an oxygen mask. They checked his blood pressure as well as his pulse.

He was alive but weak and fading. They had to get him to the mainland fast. The pilot signaled they were to take off and everyone should put their seat belts on. Then another stretcher was being ran out to the chopper.

They wouldn't.

They did.

The attempted murderer was placed right next to his victim. Looking at them side by side, it looked like an accident with two victims. Allison's palms started to sweat. She hated the thought of being this close to him. She couldn't sleep now even though sleep clawed at her eye lids.

The helicopter took off and Allison's stomach lurched from the upward movement.

The flight was fast. Before she knew it, they were landing. People were waiting for them. Lots of people. She was in no mood to interact with anyone. She was starting to get light headed and woozy. She looked over at Bryson laying beside her on the cold white stretcher, so still. Allison calmed down when she watched his chest raise up and down, signaling his breathing. She held his hand and her heart swelled when his hand tightened around hers.

The IV seemed to return color to his face. She was admiring his face when the doors of the helicopter flew open, and tons of medics rushed in. They took the murderer first then went for Bryson. She wouldn't let his had go.

"Slow down...easy." In their rush the medics didn't see Allison holding on to Bryson's hand. They slowed down as they rolled Bryson towards the hospital. Outside, the air was warm and humid against her skin. She walked next to Bryson's stretcher, keeping up with the medics pace as they pushed him into the hospital, happy he was squeezing her hand.

The bright fluorescent lights of the hospital caused Allison to turn away, because they hurt her eyes. The took him straight to the ER. Allison couldn't follow, so she waited outside for two hours pacing and worrying. She wouldn't sit down, wouldn't eat or drink anything the nurses offered her.

Relief flooded Allison when they wheeled Bryson out of the ER and headed towards his room. She took her place beside him and held his hand on the way to his room.

Once situated in his room, Allison collapsed on the chair. She was on solid ground. The buzz of other people took some getting use to. She'd been away from them for so long. As soon as she took a nap, she would call her parents, and let them know she was safe.

The doctors wanted to check her out also. They ran many tests and decided she was somewhat in shock and needed electrolytes so they put her on an IV in the room next to Bryson.

There, she fell into a heavy dreamless sleep.

When Allison woke up, she came face to face with her father, mother and best friend Samantha. They were all staring at her, giddy. When they saw she was awake, they all started talking at the same time.

"How are you-"

"How do you feel-"

"Can I get you anything-"

"How is your pillow-"

They all spoke together in a chorus, coming around Allison in a protective circle. She saw the love in her life, and felt overwhelmed. She started crying openly. Her mother sat on the bed and placed her daughters head in her lap, and stroked her hair.

"*It's OK Alli-boo, it's OK You're OK,*" said Celete in a soothing voice.

She wasn't sad, and wanted everyone to know this.

"I love you."

"I love you too Alli."

"...and I love you," said her dad

"...and I love you too," said samantha.

She cried again and before she knew it she wanted to come clean and tell the most important people in her life the truth. She felt awful having hid it and she couldn't wait to release it.

"I'm pregnant."

Confusion contorted her parents faces. Knowing surprise flashed across Samantha's.

"You are what?" asked Thomas. "I don't understand," he continued.

"I am pregnant and I'm sorry, but I am and I love him and I'm keeping the baby and I'm sorry I didn't tell you, but this is the right thing to do and I love him-" said Allison.

Celeste interrupted her daughters rant when she placed a soft finger over her lips.

"Calm down Allison. What are you talking about?"

Concerned, she pressed the call button, to alert the Nurse. She felt her daughters forehead for a fever, but she wasn't feverish. That worried Celeste, because her poor baby was hallucinating. She looked at the IV, and wondered if there was anything more than saline solution in it.

"Mom, I am calm. I am pregnant."

"When sweetie, they just brought you in last night. When could you have gotten pregnant?"

"Two and a half months ago."

That caught Celeste off guard. Allison looked at Thomas and Celeste with apprehension. She was kind of glad she was in the hospital. They wouldn't yell and be upset when she wasn't well, right?

No one said anything. Not Thomas, whose face showed a series of emotion. He went form confused to worried to disbelief, to worry, to confusion and now he sat before her, his face blank.

"Who is the father?" asked Thomas.

"Bryson Anderson Jr."

"What?" How could that be. Are you sure."

A look passed between Thomas and Celeste. One that went back to worrying about their daughters mental state. After all, she'd just been through a tough ordeal.

"Two and a half months ago, I met Bryson in Atlanta.

We hit it off and he got me pregnant." She skipped over the biology of the matter.

"Then when I came here I met him again but I didn't know I would be working with him or if I'd ever see him again."

"Why not sweetie? What kind of man gets a girl pregnant and leaves them? Is that what he did? After he found out you were pregnant, he left you, and came to the Caymans?" asked Thomas.

Heat flowed off Thomas in droves. His anger was starting to reach a boiling point.

"No, no Dad. It's a little complicated, but he left the morning after-"

"It was a one night stand?" asked Celeste in disbelief. "You don't do things like that sweetheart? Did he date rape you-"

"No, Mom." Allison began to regret saying anything.

This was reality.

She wondered if she could transport herself and Bryson back onto his island.

"Listen guys. He did not date rape me, I went willingly."

She felt so stupid.

Allison's face got red and she wanted to give up, but she pushed on. She held her stomach for strength, and continued.

"It was a one night romp, but we found each other again. We've decided to be together and--"

"Young people. What do you mean be together? You are having his baby. Has he asked you to marry him?" asked Thomas.

"Well no but-"

"But nothing--"

"Dad he's been shot, and is next door recovering. I don't think he's able to ask me to marry him-"

"Have you all talked about it?"

This was getting to be a little much for her. She was getting tired and would rather deal with this later. "These are modern times Dad, a woman can have a baby without being married."

"Not my daughter."

"What's that suppose to mean?" She didn't want to fight plus she was very hungry. Celeste sensed where this was going, and didn't want it to go any further.

"Allison needs her rest. We'll talk about this later, alright." She looked at her husband and her daughter for a truce.

"Ok, later" said Allison.

"Later," said Thomas.

She looked at the florescent lights in the hospital and thought about Bryson, she hoped he was awake, but she didn't want to ask.

"What happened?"

"Bryson was going to get some paperwork he'd left at the island, when we heard a big bang, the plane went down, and we ended up on the far side of their island. I was asleep for almost two days. He took care of me. Then he carried me over to the villa, where we stayed and waited. Then yesterday some guy came, shot Bryson in the back and tried to shoot me too."

The emotion of the events of the past few days flooded her. She got so hungry.

"Do you know when they serve dinner or breakfast or lunch? What time is it?" asked Allison.

A chuckle came from the far end of the hospital room. Everyone forgot Samantha was still there.

Well you are eating for two now. I'll go ask. If they are between meals, I'll run down to the lunchroom and get you something."

Samantha disappeared out of the room, and she was once again left alone with her parents. What now?

"So..." said Allison.

Celeste smiled. "Look, get better. We are going to be here until you're better. We'll go back with you to Atlanta. I hear our bedroom is ready. Samantha told us. Let's try and get you settled back in."

The tension started to dissipate. Thomas walked over to his daughter and gave her a kiss on her forehead.

"Welcome back Princess. We missed you. We are so happy you are back. I almost lost it when I heard."

"Lost it?" chimed Celeste. Looking at Allison she said, "Honey, he was so angry and worried, he didn't know what to do with himself. He cursed everyone, and was an all around disagreeable person."

Allison knew what her mother was talking about. Her Dad didn't handle stress well. She laughed at the memory of her dad at her little league soccer games. He would be so wound up before each and every game. During the game he would cheer the loudest if her team won, and whine the biggest if they lost. There was always a conspiracy when her team lost.

"I'm glad I'm back too. I missed you guys something terrible."

Samantha came back with roast chicken, mashed potatoes, and green beans. Her stomach growled as she smelled the food. She motioned to Sam to bring forth the food.

She dug in as soon as the tray was placed in front of her. Allison didn't know if she was hungry, or if the hospital cooked exceptionally well, but the food was delicious. The chicken, mashed potatoes, and even the vegetables were excellent.

She ate it all.

True to their word, no one left. Thomas asked the nurses for extra chairs. He told the hospital staff Samantha was their daughter so she could stay. They flipped through bad television and talked about old times. Allison ate again when dinner was served and laid back onto the reclined hospital bed, sated.

Her family was there, her best friend was there, but she longed for someone that was missing. Although he was next door, he felt like light years away. As she was dosing off, a figure in a wheel chair rolled to the door. He was cast in shadows, and through her sleepy eyes she didn't make the person out. She saw her parents and Samantha sit up straight. When she focused on him, she realized it was Bryson taking up the doorway in his wheelchair, looking at her.

# *TWENTY-ONE*

POLICE WERE STATIONED IN front of Deval "Sean" Patel's room. Allison told the medics who then told the police that he was the one who tried to kill her and Bryson. Clive Williams, the campaign manager for Ronny Ronald, Bryson's political rival, walked by and cursed under his breath. He didn't know how he would get to him now. The idiot got himself caught which put Clive in danger. He walked around the hospital floor again before attempting to gain access to the Deval's room. He walked up to one of the Officers and said,

"Hello. My name is Clive Williams and I knew Deval. Would I be able to see him?"

"No, Sir. This patient is now in police custody and we are not allowing him any visitors."

"Has he woken up?" asked Clive.

"I'm not at Liberty to say Mr.--"

"Williams."

"...Mr. Williams."

Clive thanked the Officer and walked away dejected. He should have know better than to put his trust in an idiot, like Deval "Sean" Patel. But he was the only one he knew that both hated Bryson and knew his way around an aircraft. Deval "Sean" Patel not only knew how to fly one, but knew it mechanically. If he wasn't such an idiot, he could have made a good living as a pilot.

Clive was on his way out of the hospital when he ran into Mr. and Mrs. Anderson. Great. The last people he wanted to see. He put on a forced jovial smile and addressed Bryson Sr.

"Mr. Anderson, good to see you." Clive held his hand out and Bryson Sr. shook it. Clive knew Bryson Sr. didn't care for him. Well that was an understatement. Clive knew Bryson Sr. hated him with a passion. It was probably one of the reasons, Bryson Sr. was glad his son was planning to run against his client Ronny Ronald, for Public Office.

"Clive," said Bryson Sr.

"How is Bryson Jr., I tried to see him, but I couldn't find his room."

"He's alive and doing well."

"Good, good. I hope he's back on his feet real soon. I've been looking forward and planning his defeat in the primaries next year." Clive let out a hearty chuckle not befitting the circumstances. Bryson Sr. looked at him with a curious glance.

"Well we'll see what happens. I don't know if he'll want to run anymore." Bryson Sr. and Antoinette started past Clive. The conversation was just about over.

"I hope he reconsiders. Say hi to him for me." Clive let the Anderson's pass and continued out the hospital door. He couldn't believe his luck. As long as Sean didn't wake up, he was free and clear. Bryson wouldn't run, so Ronny would definitely win the Primary. All his hard work was starting to pay off. He smiled as he walked to his car and unlocked the door. Everything was working out perfectly.

## *TWENTY-TWO*

THE TENSION IN THE air increased ten fold when everyone recognized who it was. There was shuffling of paper and bodies. Samantha stretched, walked over to Allison and gave her a peck on the cheek. She figured it was time to head out. Alli's parents didn't move. They watched Bryson roll himself in the room, not feeling an inch of sorrow for him, and the state he was in. They heard what happened to him, but all they saw and cared about was what he did to their daughter.

"Is this him?" asked Thomas. Said with such vitriol, Bryson could have been shit on the bottom of his shoe.

Holding out his hand to the man Bryson recognized as Allison's father, with the same deep penetrating eyes and nose, he said, "I'm Bryson Anderson Jr. It's a pleasure to finally meet you."

Thomas looked at Bryson's outstretched hand for a second longer than necessary, before shaking it. Allison sat up in bed as Bryson rolled over to her mother, and introduced himself.

The buzz of the muted television was the only sound in the room. Allison felt like she was twelve years old again, sitting in the principals office, while her parents received the run down of everything she'd done wrong in the past few hours.

"Did you date rape my daughter?" The words flew out of Celeste's mouth before Allison could stop it.

"Oh my God Mom." Allison's cheeks got as red as tomatoes, and an embarrassed and apologetic look tried to reach Bryson.

But he wasn't looking at her. He was considering Celeste, carefully. If he messed this up, it would mean a very stressed relationship for the foreseeable future. He didn't know why, but he was coming into this a step behind.

He was already under. Bryson loved to be the underdog in business transactions. It meant, your opponent never saw you coming, underestimated you and usually made small but expensive mistakes. Take Sun-splash Resort. He was able to get in and get the board of directors on his side, because Sean was busy underestimating him.

This was different.

Although no money was involved, the stakes were higher.

"Mrs. Caine. I love Allison so much it hurts. Every second of every day I am with her, my heart is happy, every second I'm not, I am miserable. She holds my heart in her hands. I swear on our unborn child I did not date rape Allison."

The sweet words made Allison smile behind him, and softened Celeste slightly.

Thomas didn't care how sweet his words were.

"First you get my daughter pregnant and leave her like a common whore, then you almost get her killed twice, and you think you can make it all better with words?"

A wrong done to his daughter was a wrong done to Thomas himself.

Bryson was at a loss for words. He didn't know what if anything he could say. His shoulder started to throb and fatigue was engulfing his body.

"Mr. Caine, I did not leave Allison. That was a big misunderstanding that we've since cleared up." He looked over to Allison for support.

"That's true Dad."

"I would never put Allison in danger, knowingly. I feel terrible that she has a scratch on her. I don't have any other answers. I want to know what happened as much as you do. Look, I came to see how Allison was doing. I heard she was awake."

He then turned all of his attention to Allison.

"Hi Sunshine, how are you?"

Everyone and everything in the room disappeared, and it was just the two of them again. The buzz of the television and the machines she was hooked to, disappeared as well as the disapproving glares of her parents.

"Good, now that you're here."

He rubbed her arm, and was engulfed by her deep penetrating eyes.

"How's the arm and the leg?"

"Excellent. It could have been a lot worse." His smile was goofy and sexy as hell, to Allison.

They were both aware of mumbling behind them. Neither of them bothered to find out what was going on. They both reveled in each others safety.

"...we need to make sure the baby's okay," said Celeste.

That drew Allison's attention to the conversation going on without her.

"What? What are you all talking about."

"You've just gone through a big ordeal. We have to make sure your baby is okay. Have they checked it out completely."

Allison was trying to avoid this confrontation. She hadn't steeled herself to the possibility that something would be wrong with her baby. The thought alone scared her.

One thing at a time.

Her baby had to be there. Everything was working out the way it should, there wasn't a need to even check.

"Mom, I'm sure everything is fine."

" I'm sure it is too sweetie, but we must make sure."

Intense fear bit at Allison.

What if?

She tried to tamp it down, but the acrid taste in her mouth refused to go away. Bryson realized Alli's alarm and was immediately concerned.

"It's fine Sunshine, I think your Mom's right."

Celeste heard this. One point in the pro Bryson column. If a young man immediately recognized that she was right, then he couldn't be all that bad. Without wasting any time, Celeste walked out to the nurse's station, and came back with Alli's nurse for the night.

"My daughter is pregnant, and we want to make sure the baby is okay after all she's just been through."

"Certainly. We were unaware you are expecting," said the nurse as she leafed through the medical chart on the foot of Allison's bed.

"Let me take some blood and I'll be back with the ultrasound machine."

The nurse left the room and was back before anyone could think of what to say.

"Alright, here we go." The nurse worked methodically to hook up the ultrasound machine. With the tools she placed on the counter, she took a needle and drew blood from a tube already in Allison's arm.

"Doing good," said the nurse.

Then she turned on the machine. She reached for the cold gel and turned to Mr. and Ms. Caine.

"Can you two please give us a minute. She will be done soon."

Thomas and Celeste dragged themselves out of the room, walking slower than Allison had ever seen them move. After they left and the door was closed behind them, Allison turned to the nurse and gave her a grateful smile.

"Thanks."

"No problem hon. I could tell they were making you a little nervous."

Allison wasn't ready for the gel to be so cold. She braced, as the nurse rubbed the cold gel around her stomach. The screen went on and everyone still left in the room, the nurse, Allison and Bryson, glanced up at the black and white screen.

Allison and Bryson didn't know what they should be looking for, but they looked nonetheless.

The nurse used the tool while looking at the screen to look for the baby.

She looked and looked. Moved the tool around Alison's stomach where the baby should have been. She zoomed in and zoomed out. She focused in and focused out. After eight minutes of searching, she turned off the machine and looked at the couple.

"I don't see anything."

"I don't understand," said Bryson.

"The baby is gone. There is no more baby."

The words Allison had been dreading since she woke up on the beach days earlier were coming true, but it wasn't how she thought it would be.

She felt empty.

She felt numb. She felt a gaping void where none had been before. Sadness overtook her. She'd lost it. Her baby. She'd lost it. Running the words through her mind, turning it over and trying to understand what it meant, got her nowhere. She felt like it was her fault, like she wasn't strong enough somehow, and she was unable to care for her young. She felt like a failure.

Intense pain made Allison contract her body. She felt the pain physically and emotionally. That man did succeed in killing her baby, and she was useless to protect it.

She felt like a total and utter failure.

Bryson was sitting looking at the nurse bewildered.

"It's gone? How could that be?" asked Bryson.

"I'm sorry, but sometimes that happens. Miscarriages are very common. But hey, it's always fun to try again."

The nurse picked up the pace in getting her equipment together to leave. She saw the sorrow in both of their faces, and wanted out of the room.

Bryson glanced at Allison and placed her hands in his. His heart was broken. He had plans for his family. His chest literally hurt. He felt he was unable to protect his family. He was ashamed that he was flat on his face while his Allison had to defend herself against Sean. He stared at her and was proud of her strength.

But what about him? Was he strong enough? This was the family he'd long for and now it was gone.

"I'm sorry," he said.

"It's alright."

"I wish this didn't happen. I wish junior was still growing." He rubbed her stomach and looked at her. "But the nurse is right. It would be fun to try again."

Allison smiled and hugged him with wet hot tears in her eyes.

"How about we get to know each other a little better first."

"I think we know enough about each other. So, you went to a bookstore after playing hookie in school? What's the sense, you might as well have stayed in school. I've really got to show you how to be a bad girl."

"You heard that."

"Yeah, you wouldn't stop talking. All I wanted to do was take a nap, but you just kept on yapping on and on, droning on and on and on and on--"

"I get it," said Allison laughing.

"Will you Marry Me?"

"Huh?"

"Will you Marry me? Is something wrong with your ears?" He used his right index finger and tried to stick it in Allison's ear.

"Hey quit it."

"So?"

"So, what?...Oh yeah. Yes."

"Yes what?

"I'll marry you."

Bryson reached in the seat of his wheelchair and retrieved a white twistie tie, the one that keeps bread fresh, molded it around Allison's ring finger and twisted it so it looked like an engagement ring with a diamond.

"Oh my, it's beautiful. I don't know what to say. Ow."

"Sorry." He loosed the twist tie around her finger slightly.

"I was just kidding. It didn't hurt that much."

"I plan never to hurt you again, for any reason."

"Hey, what are you doing?" asked Allison.

Bryson lifted his weight up and slid on to the bed beside Allison.

"Move over."

"Hey this is my bed, go back to your own bed."

"Why don't you make me."

Allison snuggled up to her man in the twin sized hospital bed, both of them uncomfortable with half their bodies off the bed, pushing and shoving each other and laughing like school children.

When Alison's parents looked into the room, half sorry and half happy at the news the nurse conveyed to them, they saw the couple embracing on the bed. Celeste closed the door behind her as she took her husbands hands, and walked away.

"Mr. Anderson! I've been looking for you. What are you doing here. You should be in your room." Bryson's nurse came into the room after passing Allison's parent's in the hallway, and learning his location.

"Oh no," said Bryson to Allison. "Hide me, nurse Ratchett is looking for me."

"I heard that Mr. Anderson."

Giggling, Allison said, "Baby, I don't have anywhere to hide you, she already saw you."

"I need you back in your wheelchair Sir, you have wounds on your body we need you to get better. "

"I'm Fine."

"No you're not." The nurse moved to the bed and held Bryson's hand as she guided him into his wheelchair. He gave Allison a puppy dog look as he was wheeled out.

Allison's head fell back and connected with the pillow. She stared at the florescent lights without seeing them. Less than a week ago, she was on a flight from Atlanta, pregnant and angry, trying to save her job. Now she was engaged to a man she thought she would never see again. Life had a funny way of working out.

Life dragged her in a total opposite direction than she was planning to go, but somehow, it worked out better than she could have imagined.

*I wonder what's going to happen next week*, she thought, before falling into a deep dreamless sleep.

## THE END

Claimed By Desire

KayAnna Kirby

## *ABOUT THE AUTHOR*

KayAnna Kirby is a little introverted, but fun (when she decides to loosen up a bit.) She fell in love with reading in elementary school and continued to devour books whether she worked for a toy store, retail clothing store, International Banking Company, or sold cars or cosmetics.

KayAnna has a four year old daughter who is going on sixteen. KayAnna lives with her wonderful husband Gregory, who has to put up with KayAnna constantly forgetting their wedding anniversary. (He forgets too.)

She was told specifically *not* to adopt her dog Titan from the pound, because the employees said he was "peculiar". After six years, she must reluctantly agree.

KayAnna works with her husband (and no, neither of them have tried to kill the other...yet) in a suburb outside of Atlanta, where they currently live.

Her debut novel, Claimed By Desire, releases May 2011.